The Balloons
of Oaxaca

The Balloons of Oaxaca

By
Barry Head

Illustrated by
Noël Chilton

Library of Congress Control Number:		2006906809
ISBN 10:	Hardcover	1-4257-2660-7
	Softcover	1-4257-2659-3
ISBN 13:	Hardcover	978-1-4257-2660-7
	Softcover	978-1-4257-2659-1

This book was printed in the United States of America.

To order additional copies of this book, contact:
Xlibris Corporation
1-888-795-4274
www.Xlibris.com
Orders@Xlibris.com
35398

For
Adrian

And in loving memory of
Fred Rogers
Guide, Philosopher and Friend

Chapter One

In the city of Oaxaca, in a country called Mexico, there lives a boy whose name is Utuyu.

Those are strange names, aren't they? They're easy names to say, though, and I'll tell you how to say them. You say Oaxaca the way you'd say Wa-HA-ka, with the HA a little louder than the rest. Wa-HA-ka. If you try saying it, you'll find it's not so hard. It looks strange when you write it out on paper, because it comes from an old language that is very different from yours and mine.

You say Mexico like you'd say MEK-si-co. You may already know how to say that one. As for the boy's name, it comes from another old language, and you say it the way you'd say Oo-too-YOO, with the YOO a little louder than the rest. In the old language of Utuyu's people, his name means "sky."

At the time of this story, Utuyu is about six years old. I say "about six years old," because Utuyu didn't know exactly how old he was. Neither did anyone else. His mother and father might have known how old Utuyu was, but nobody knew where his mother and father were.

Many different people looked after Utuyu before he was able to look after himself, but none of those people had room to look after him for very long. Even if they'd had enough room for him, they wouldn't have had enough food to keep feeding him for very long. They had to feed themselves, and they had many children of their own to feed as well. That's why, when Utuyu was about six years old, there came a day when no one would look after him anymore.

The last person who looked after Utuyu was a woman named Ita, which you say the way you'd say EE-ta, with the EE a little louder than the rest. Ita had seven other children of her own to look after. Except for Ita's little baby, all the children slept together on thin, grass mats on the hard, dirt floor of one of the two small rooms in Ita's house. The house was up in a valley in what are called The Mountains to the North. The Mountains to the North rise above the city of Oaxaca, and you can see them from a long way away.

For most of the year, the sun was hot in the mountains, and the house was warm, but there was a time in the winter months when the nights became cold. Then, all the children, except the baby, slept in a bundle in the middle of the floor, keeping each other warm. The baby slept close to her mother, and that's how the two of them kept warm. In the hot weather, the children slept around the edges of the room, against the walls. Utuyu didn't mind sleeping either way—in the middle of the room in a bundle, or around the edges against the walls. What he liked was sleeping with a lot of other people around him, hearing them breathing, and murmuring, and snoring whenever he happened to wake up in the middle of the night.

Some nights, there were more children sleeping in the room than on other nights. This was because Ita's children often walked down the mountain to the city of Oaxaca. The city was much too far away for them to come back to sleep in Ita's house the same night. They would start out when the sun went down, and if they walked all the way, the sun would be high overhead the next day by the time they got to the city. Walking home again took the children longer, because they had to walk up the mountain instead of down, and of course they walked more slowly going uphill. They also usually brought things back from the city, and carrying their packages and bags slowed them down, too.

When Utuyu first came to Ita's house, only her four oldest children went to the city. As time went by, though, all Ita's children—except the baby, of course—were old enough to go. Usually, they would be away from the house for many days and nights, so Utuyu was often at the house alone with Ita and her baby. Whenever Ita's children came back to the house from the city, she greeted them the same way. "Everyone safe and sound?" she'd say.

The children always came back from the city with new stories. Utuyu wanted to know everything about what they'd been doing while they were away. He liked hearing again and again about their long, slow walk, about the birds and animals they'd seen, about the fruits they'd found to eat along the way, and about the other grownups and other children who were walking to the city as well. Somewhere along the road, Ita's children told him, there was a pool in the river where everyone stopped for a while. The grownups would sit in the shade of the trees, talking and eating, while the children splashed in the water to cool off. Then everyone would move on again down the mountains toward the city.

Ita's children didn't always have to walk all the way to the city and back. They told Utuyu how, if they were lucky, the driver of an old truck would stop and let them get in the back. When that happened on the way to the city, they said, they would sit in the back and shout as loud as they could as the truck turned and twisted down the mountain, around the sharp, steep curves. They'd bang on the little window behind the driver, and the driver knew their banging meant they wanted him to make the truck go faster—and he would. When he did, and brought the truck around another steep curve, they'd all shout louder still.

It was hard for Utuyu to imagine what it was like in the city of Oaxaca. From the children's stories, it sounded like the whole place was full of cars and trucks and people almost all the time, day and night. They said there was music everywhere, and food of more different kinds than you could name. They said it was noisy, with loud church bells and things called fireworks that suddenly went off with a BANG! and made you jump when they exploded in colors above your head.

Once, Ita's children brought back three balloons on strings—a bright, yellow one with a face on it, a bright, red one with some words on it, and a shiny, silver one in the shape of a dog. The children said there were lots and lots of people selling balloons in the central square of the city, holding onto enormous bunches of them. The bunches were so big you couldn't see the person holding them anymore. One thing Utuyu learned about the three balloons the children brought back to Ita's house was that if you let go of the string, the balloon on the other end would fly away into the sky. That's what happened when he was playing with the red one and let go of the string by mistake. Up and away it went, until it got so small in the blue sky that he couldn't see it anymore, and it never came back. The yellow one and the one in the shape of a dog stayed up against the ceiling of Ita's house for a long time, but then they seemed to get tired of staying there and slowly came down to the ground. After that, the balloons didn't try to fly away anymore.

The children brought something else back from the city whenever they returned—pocketsful of coins, which they gave to Ita. Ita let Utuyu play with the coins, and that's how he learned their names and how to count all the way to 50.

Utuyu wanted to go to the city with all the others. He wanted to see it for himself, to see if the stories the children were telling him were really true. If they were true, then the walk to the city had to be truly wonderful. Certainly life in Oaxaca itself, once you got there, sounded better than carrying heavy buckets of water from the river, one at a time. It sounded better than gathering armfuls of prickly wood for the fire. It certainly sounded a whole lot better to Utuyu than sitting still for hours, mashing corn with a stone until his arms ached so much that he thought they were about to fall off—but of course arms can't do that, can they?

When there was no work to do, which wasn't very often, Utuyu had a favorite place he'd go to where he could be by himself. No one else ever seemed to go there. It was a place where rocks had fallen into a pile, and if you turned over the right rocks, you'd always find scorpions there. Utuyu knew that scorpions could sting you and make you sick, but that only happened if you got too close to them, which Utuyu never did. He liked the way the scorpions looked—black and shiny, with their sharp tails curled over their backs. He liked touching one with a stick and seeing it try to sting the wood.

"You silly scorpion!" Utuyu would say. "Sticks can't feel your sting!"

At times, Utuyu imagined a scorpion was answering him. Once, one of them seemed to say, *You are the silly one. We sting whatever there is to sting. Doing our stinging feels good.*

When Utuyu pushed two of the scorpions together, they tried to sting each other.

"That's *really* stupid of you," Utuyu told them. "Now look what you've done!"

We sting, one of the scorpions seemed to say. *That's what we do. What you do is up to you. You'll find out.*

The times Utuyu liked best at Ita's house were when all her children were there, and something would happen to make people from all over the place come and visit. They didn't come only for a little while and then go away again. They'd come bringing bags and bundles, and they'd stay and stay and stay. At nights, they all seemed to be in a good mood, and they'd dance and tell stories and sing.

It was the singing part of these times that Utuyu liked the most of all. When he was alone with Ita and her baby, when all her other children had gone to the city, Ita would teach him songs that she said their people had been singing for longer than anyone could remember. Utuyu found the songs easy to learn. When he and Ita would sing them together, she'd clap her hands and shake her head.

"None of my children learned songs as fast as you do," she told Utuyu one day when they were singing. "And none of them has as sweet a voice as you have."

That, of course, made Utuyu feel good. Whenever the people came from all over to stay, Ita would ask Utuyu to sing to them. When he did, *everyone* clapped their hands and shook their heads.

Chapter Two

For a long time, Ita told Utuyu he was too young to go to the city with the others. He didn't argue about it, because he learned, as soon as he moved into Ita's house, that nobody argued with Ita about anything. You did what she told you to do, and you did it when she told you to do it. So, when one day Ita finally told Utuyu that it was time for him to leave the house and go to the city, he didn't argue about that, either. In fact, Utuyu didn't want to argue about it, even though Ita told him he was to go to city for good. She didn't say that he could never come back again, but she did say that she wasn't going to look after him anymore, and that he was going to have to start looking after himself. That was fine by Utuyu. He felt quite sure that he didn't need anyone to look after him, and now, at last, he was going to get to see the city of Oaxaca for himself. He'd find out whether all the things Ita's children had been telling him were true.

The next time Ita's children went down the mountain, Utuyu went with them. It was getting dark when they got ready to leave the house. Ita gave Utuyu a package of the flat bread she was always making, the bread she made from the corn he had helped mash. The bread was all he took with him, except for the shirt and shorts and sandals he was wearing. He thanked Ita for the bread and said goodbye. He didn't see Ita standing in the doorway, her hands on her hips, shaking her head slowly from side to side as she watched him go. Utuyu didn't see her, not because it was dark, but because he didn't look back.

They walked and walked. At least the other children walked, but Utuyu often had to run to keep up with them. His legs were much shorter than theirs, so he had to make his go faster.

To their left, the sky became purple instead of black.

"Is it still a long way to Oaxaca?" Utuyu asked.

"Yes," said the children. "A long way."

They went on walking. The sky became dark blue.

"Are we almost there?" Utuyu asked.

"No," said the children.

They went on walking. The sky became a lighter blue.

"Are we ever going to get to Oaxaca?" Utuyu asked.

"Yes," said the children.

They went on walking. The sky became yellow.

"Now are we almost there?" Utuyu asked.

"No," said the children.

The sun came up over the mountains, and still they walked. The day became hot. Utuyu's legs were tired, and he was already hungry and thirsty.

"I want to stop for a while," Utuyu said. "Okay?"

"Yes," said the children.

"Will you wait for me?" Utuyu asked.

"No," said the children. "You can catch up with us at the pool in the river."

Utuyu sat down beside the path. The other children went on, leaving him alone as they disappeared from sight around the next turn. He unwrapped the package of bread and tried to eat a piece, but his mouth was too dry to swallow it. He needed something to drink. Looking around, he saw a line of dark green plants a little distance away, and he recognized them as the same kind of plants that grew beside the river where he went to get pails of water for Ita.

Maybe the plants know something, Utuyu thought, and when he went to where they were growing, there, sure enough, was a little trickle of water running beneath them. He flung himself down on his stomach, pushed the plants aside, stuck out his tongue to reach the water, and—

"Ay!" he shouted. Not more than two inches from his nose was a large, shiny, black scorpion, its pointed tail arched over its back.

Utuyu jerked his head away from the water in a hurry and sat back on his heels.

"Bad!" Utuyu said to the scorpion. "You are bad to scare me like that!"

And you are a silly boy to go looking with your tongue instead of your eyes, the scorpion seemed to say.

"Go away now," said Utuyu. "I'm thirsty. Let me drink."

Drink then, said the scorpion, walking slowly into the leaves of the plants, *but silly boys like you won't last long in Oaxaca. Remember me. Keep your eyes open in the front of your head. Keep your ears open on the sides of your head. Keep your tongue in your mouth, like a bird in a cage.*

Then the scorpion was gone.

Utuyu drank from the water and finished the piece of bread. When he was done, he walked on down the mountain. The path turned into a wider track. From both sides, grownups and children from other valleys joined in the long walk to Oaxaca. They all had bundles on their backs, and some of the women had babies tied on in front of them as well. They spoke to him, and Utuyu tried to ask them how far they still had to go, but they spoke a different language that didn't sound anything like his own. They were friendly, though, and smiled. Utuyu was glad not to be walking alone anymore.

The sun climbed higher, and the day grew hotter. The track ahead kept uncurling like a long ribbon that some giant had dropped on the ground, but the hills were lower now. A rumbling far behind them made everyone turn around, and when they saw the cloud of dust approaching, they began walking back the way they had come, waving and shouting.

Why walk back uphill, Utuyu wondered, *when you were going to have to walk back down again?* He didn't follow the others and stayed right where he was. Out of the cloud of dust came an old truck, and Utuyu understood. Everyone was hoping to be the first to get to the truck and find a place to ride in the back. By staying where he was, he had made himself the last in line, the last by far.

The truck, though, did not stop for anyone. The back was already full of people. The driver kept shaking his head and slowly continuing down the hill, leaving the walkers behind to walk back down again. Utuyu stood alone by the side of the track, watching the truck get nearer.

Remember me, he heard the scorpion saying inside his head. Pretending he had hurt his foot, Utuyu limped slowly into the middle of the track and sat down—right there in the middle of the road. The truck came to a stop in front of him. The driver leaned out of his window and shouted something, waving with one hand for Utuyu to get out of the way.

Keep your tongue in your mouth, like a bird in a cage, Utuyu heard the scorpion saying.

Utuyu didn't move from where he sat. He stared at the driver and didn't say a thing. The driver shouted and waved at him again. The people in the back leaned out around the sides of the truck to see what was going on. One of them said something to the driver, who shrugged his shoulders. A tall boy jumped out of the back of the truck, took Utuyu by the arms, and lifted him to his feet.

"Come on!" the boy said in Utuyu's own language. "It's lucky for you that you're so small!"

Forgetting to limp, Utuyu ran with the boy to the truck, and the boy pushed him up over back. The people inside pulled him in, clapping and laughing. The boy, himself, jumped in, slapped the side of the truck to tell the driver could start again, and away they went.

Down and down they went. Before long, the truck came up behind Ita's children. Utuyu waved at them as the truck passed.

"Wait for us at the pool in the river!" shouted one of Ita's children.

"We're not stopping there," the tall boy told Utuyu.

"No!" Utuyu shouted to Ita's children. "You can catch up with me in Oaxaca!"

Ita's children waved and disappeared into the cloud of dust behind the truck.

Utuyu was asleep when the truck passed the pool in the river, so he didn't see all the grownups sitting in the shade of the trees while the children splashed in the water. He was still sleeping as the hills turned into one long slope downhill, and as the sharp curves in the road smoothed out into more gentle bends. What woke him up was the sound of excited talk around him, and when he looked to see what was going on, there was the city of Oaxaca ahead. To Utuyu, it seemed an endless place of rooftops all crowded together. Here and there, taller, dome-shaped buildings rose above the others. Above them all, from the middle of the sky, the bright, hot sun shone down on everything.

Chapter Three

The truck stopped on the edge of the city, and everyone got out. They gathered up their packages, waved goodbye to the truck driver, and started walking off in different directions. With a toot of his horn, the driver drove his truck into the stream of other trucks and busses and cars that were swirling around. In a moment, Utuyu couldn't tell which truck was which. He stood there, wondering what to do next.

"Where are you going?" asked the tall boy who had helped him into the back of the truck.

"I'm going to Oaxaca," said Utuyu.

"This is Oaxaca," said the boy. "Where are you going now?"

"I'm not going anywhere," said Utuyu. "I'm staying here."

"Right here? Where you're standing?" asked the boy, laughing.

Utuyu hadn't thought about anything more than just going to Oaxaca, so he didn't know what to say.

"Who do you know here?" asked the boy.

"No one," said Utuyu.

"No one?" asked the boy. "No one at all?"

"No," said Utuyu.

"Where are you going to sleep tonight?" asked the boy.

"Wherever," said Utuyu with a shrug of his shoulders that was meant to show that he didn't really care where he slept. It wasn't a very good shrug, though, because the boy's questions were making Utuyu feel uneasy inside.

"Who's going to look after you?" asked the boy.

Utuyu shrugged a shrug that was worse than the first one. It fact, it was hardly a shrug at all. "I'm going to look after myself," he said, but his voice sounded very small.

The boy looked at him and shook his head. "You don't know anything, do you?" said the boy. "I bet you don't even know your name!"

"I do, too!" said Utuyu. He felt a little angry now, and that made him feel better again.

"So, what is it?" asked the boy.

"None of your business," said Utuyu.

"Who were the kids you waved at from the truck?" asked the boy.

"Ita's children," said Utuyu.

"Your brothers and sisters?" asked the boy. "Are they going to look after you?"

"They're not my brothers and sisters, and I already told you I'm going to look after myself," said Utuyu. "Stop asking me so many questions and leave me alone!"

"Leave you alone?" said the boy with a laugh. "I don't have to leave you alone, because you're already alone!"

Utuyu looked at all the trucks and busses and cars whirling past, at all the streets that went off in every direction, at all the houses and shops that all looked the same. The boy was right: Utuyu knew he couldn't stay standing where he was standing forever. He also didn't want to go on seeming stupid. There seemed to be no way across the road, because of all the trucks and busses and cars that never stopped, so, without looking back at the boy, Utuyu started walking along the sidewalk on his side of the road.

"Where are you going?" shouted the boy.

Utuyu didn't answer. He kept on walking.

"Going back home?" shouted the boy.

Utuyu shook his head and kept on walking.

"Good luck!" shouted the boy, and Utuyu kept on walking.

He hadn't gone far before the sidewalk ended at another stream of trucks and busses and cars that blocked his way. There were other people standing at the end of the sidewalk, too, and Utuyu stood there with them, watching to see what they were going to do. Suddenly, for no reason Utuyu could figure out, all the traffic stopped, and the people went across the street. Utuyu went with them. *So that's what you do,* he thought. *You look for the people who can stop everything, and then you go with them. That's not so hard.* It always seemed to work, and soon Utuyu had crossed many busy streets.

There was something that puzzled Utuyu, though. All the people in the streets were talking to one another, but Utuyu couldn't understand a word of what they were saying. He hadn't been able to understand some of the other people who had been walking out of the mountains to Oaxaca, but it hadn't mattered. Many of them couldn't understand each other, either. In Oaxaca, though, everyone seemed to understand everyone else, but Utuyu couldn't understand anything.

That was a mystery.

Chapter Four

By the time the sun was lower in the sky and the air was cooler, Utuyu was walking through a place where everyone had put food out on stands. The stories Ita's children told were true. There were more kinds of food than he had ever seen before. The sight of all the food made Utuyu hungry, and that made him think of the rest of Ita's bread, and that made him wonder where it had gone. He didn't have it anymore. He'd left it in the back of the truck.

Utuyu watched the people who were taking food from the stands. They always gave back coins like the ones Ita's children brought home. But where had Ita's children found the coins, Utuyu wondered? Where did the coins come from? Who made them? And what happened if you didn't have any coins and so you couldn't give any back?

A woman was sitting on a stool behind a pile of the flat bread Ita was always making. Utuyu went up to her and held out his hand. The woman said something to him, which, of course, he didn't understand, so he just kept holding out his hand. The woman got angry and shouted at him. Utuyu didn't understand what she shouted, but he understood right away what it meant.

A man on a street corner was standing beside a wagon, calling out something to the people who passed. Some of the people stopped, and the man handed them something that Utuyu had never seen before, but whatever it was, it smelled good and made him hungrier. The people were giving the man coins, too, and then walking away, eating whatever it was the man had given them. Utuyu went up to the man and held out his hand. The man looked at him and then looked away, calling out to the people who passed. Utuyu kept holding out his hand, but the man never looked at him again.

There was a place that had fruits of many kinds for everyone to see. Utuyu knew what many of the fruits were, because he'd eaten them before. There were mangos and papayas and bananas and avocados, and the sight of them made Utuyu's mouth water. People were crowding around the place, all touching the fruits at the same time, picking some out and putting some back. Hands were flying everywhere. A banana and an avocado lay on the ground among the people's feet, and before anyone could step on them, Utuyu wriggled through the people's legs, grabbed the banana and the avocado, and wriggled out of the people's legs in the other direction.

So that's what you do, Utuyu thought. *You go to places where there are lots of people, and you pick up what falls down. That isn't so hard.*

Utuyu was beginning to feel pleased with himself. He'd been in the back of a truck to Oaxaca, he was already able to walk around Oaxaca, and he'd found a way to eat in Oaxaca that didn't need coins. This Oaxaca place was okay, he thought. What next?

What was next was that he came to the end of a sidewalk again, and for once there were no people standing around who could make the traffic stop. Utuyu had no idea how to do that by himself. *Maybe someone will come along who knows how,* he thought, *so I'll just stay here until they do.* Although no one did come, the trucks and busses and cars suddenly stopped all by themselves. Another mystery.

Utuyu started across the street, eating his banana, when around the corner, out of nowhere, like lightning, roared a yellow truck. If a hand hadn't grabbed him by the back of his shirt and yanked him backwards, that moment could have been Utuyu's last moment in Oaxaca—or, for that matter, Utuyu's last moment anywhere. Utuyu looked to see who was holding him by his shirt. It was the tall boy again.

"You were doing okay until then, kid," the boy said, "but you got to keep your eyes open in your head."

In his mind, Utuyu could hear the scorpion saying, *"Silly boys like you won't last long in Oaxaca. Remember me."*

The yellow truck had given Utuyu a terrible scare. He sat on the curb of the sidewalk, breathing hard and unable to say anything. He felt he was about to cry, but he tried hard not to.

"Look at your banana!" said the tall boy. The banana was out there in the street, and there wasn't much left of it. So many wheels were running over it that all Utuyu could see were flashes of the banana's yellow skin between the tires.

"You want to end up like that?" asked the tall boy.

Utuyu shook his head, and then there was nothing he could do to stop some tears from falling out of his eyes. He tried to push the tears back in as fast as they came out, but they kept squeezing out between his fingers.

"You didn't have to pull me so hard," he said behind his fingers and with a big sniff.

"What?" said the tall boy, staring down at him.

"I said you didn't have to pull me so hard!" said Utuyu, looking in the other direction.

"I didn't have to pull you at all," said the boy. "I could have let you get squashed." He slapped his hands together. "Just like that!"

"What are you doing following me around, anyway?" Utuyu asked.

"I wanted to see what a dumb kid like you was going to do in a place like this," said the boy. "For a while I was thinking you weren't so dumb after all, but now I know you're even dumber than I was thinking."

Utuyu couldn't think of anything to say to that.

"So, dummy, what are you going to do now?"

"Stop calling me dummy," said Utuyu.

"You said your name was none of my business," said the boy, "so I get to call you whatever I want."

"My name is Utuyu," Utuyu said.

"Sky Boy, huh?" said the tall boy, because, as you may remember, Utuyu means "sky" in the old language of Utuyu's people.

"And you?" asked Utuyu. "What's your name?"

"Gabriel," said the boy.

"Gabriel?" said Utuyu. "I never heard that before. I'll bet it doesn't mean anything at all."

"It's the name Father Juan gave me," said Gabriel. "It doesn't have to mean anything."

"Who's Father Juan, anyway?" Utuyu asked.

"Maybe I'll let you meet him one day," said Gabriel. "That is, if you don't go and get yourself squashed before. So, like I said, where do you think you're going now?"

Utuyu didn't know what to say.

"No idea, huh?" said Gabriel. "I didn't think so."

"I do too know where I'm going," said Utuyu.

"I'll bet you don't!" said Gabriel.

"I'll bet I do!" said Utuyu.

"So, where?" said Gabriel.

Gabriel, of course, was right. Utuyu didn't have any idea where he was going. How could he know where he was going, when he didn't know where he was to begin with? But Utuyu didn't want Gabriel to keep on thinking he was dumb, so he said:

"I'm going to the place where all the balloons are."

Gabriel looked at him, a little bit surprised. "That's a good idea!" he said. "How did you come up with that one?" But then Gabriel said, "So, point the way."

Naturally, Utuyu had no idea in which direction to point, but he tried to look as if he did and stuck out his arm and forefinger toward the sunset. He watched Gabriel out of the corner of his eye so see if he was right.

Gabriel burst into laughter. "Good try!" he said, punching Utuyu on the shoulder. "If you went that way, Sky Boy, you'd get to . . . . Who knows where you'd get to! Maybe Mexico City, or somewhere like that! Maybe in a hundred years or so! Come on, follow me." Gabriel started off in a completely different direction than where Utuyu had pointed. "And hold my hand when we're crossing streets, will you?" said Gabriel. "I'm not here to scrape up squashed bananas."

Chapter Five

There have been many times in my life when, like Utuyu, I pretended I knew the answer to something I didn't know the answer to at all. No one likes to feel dumb. At least, I certainly don't. I'll tell you something I've learned, though: No one knows everything, but everyone knows something that someone else doesn't know. The more of those things we can learn from other people, the smarter we get. It may seem strange, but one of the best ways to get smart is to say, "I don't know." Gabriel knew lots of things about the city of Oaxaca that Utuyu didn't know. Utuyu had a lot of getting smarter to do.

When Gabriel started off through the streets, Utuyu had to run to keep up. The only times Gabriel slowed down were when they came to a street they had to cross. Gabriel explained how the traffic lights worked.

"When it's red," he said, "don't even try to get across. You'll be squashed for sure. When it's green, it means you only *might* get squashed. You've got to look everywhere."

Some streets didn't have a traffic light. Utuyu asked Gabriel what somebody was supposed to do then.

"In your case, Sky Boy," Gabriel told Utuyu, "cross with an old woman if there's one around. Old women don't get squashed so much."

After crossing many, many streets, Gabriel turned a corner and stopped. Utuyu stopped, too. He'd have stopped with or without Gabriel, because he'd never seen anything like the sight in front of him. He didn't have any idea what he was looking at.

They had come to the main square in the middle of the city. It was a place of enormous trees and crowds of people walking around, but the first thing Utuyu noticed was the balloons. How could there be so many balloons in the world? Everywhere he looked there were huge clumps of balloons, some of them staying still, and some of them moving about as though the wind were blowing them. There were balloons of every color Utuyu had ever seen, and there were balloons of colors he had never seen before. There were balloons of every shape. Some looked like the dog balloon Ita's children had brought back, and others looked like cats, tigers, fish and airplanes. Some of the balloons had faces. Some had writing on them. Just a single clump of balloons was more balloons than Utuyu could imagine, but there wasn't just one clump. There were clumps everywhere, and then more clumps everywhere else.

"Come on!" said Gabriel, but Utuyu didn't feel ready to move from where he was. What he saw in front of him was such a strange, new world that he needed time to think about it. Gabriel grabbed Utuyu's hand.

"Don't just stand there like somebody stupid, Sky Boy," he said. "Come on!"

Utuyu yanked his hand away, shook his head, and squatted down on his heels against a wall. He wasn't about to go anywhere with anyone, and that included with Gabriel.

"Then stay there like an old piece of stone, if that's what you want to do," said Gabriel. "I've got things to do." Gabriel walked into the crowd of people and was gone.

When you're about six years old, you're still small, and grownups look very big. When you're about six years old, and, what's more, you're squatting down on your heels . . . well, you're hardly any size at all. Grownups look like giants. Utuyu's head only came up to the knees that passed by him, and there were hundreds and hundreds of knees going back and forth in front of his eyes. Except for the jeans that went by on some knees, the rest of the clothes that passed weren't like any clothes Utuyu had seen up in The Mountains to the North. There were fancy pants and fancy skirts on the knees, and there were shorts that didn't cover the knees at all. Those knees went by in nothing more than skin. There were so many knees around him that Utuyu couldn't see the balloons anymore.

If you'd been a bird high up in one of the tall trees in the middle of the square just then, this is what you would have seen through the branches: You would have looked down on a large, open place with buildings around all the sides holding it in. Most of the buildings had arches at the bottom, and under the arches you would have seen people sitting at tables talking and eating and drinking. Because it was getting dark, you'd have seen lights everywhere, especially bright lights under the arches where the people were sitting at the tables. In the middle of the square, you'd have seen a mass of hats and heads and shoulders, and among them, popping up like huge flowers, you'd have seen the great clumps of balloons. If you'd been a bird with really sharp eyes, you might have seen a tiny, dark smudge against the bottom of one of the buildings, a smudge that didn't move at all, a smudge that was almost hidden by the mass of people.

That smudge would have been Utuyu, squatting down on his heels and wondering what to do next.

Chapter Six

Utuyu stayed right where he was, down on his heels against the wall at one edge of the square, and he stayed there for a long time.

"Maybe Gabriel will come back and find me," he thought. "He'll know what I should do next."

Utuyu thought about that, and it didn't seem a good idea. To begin with, maybe Gabriel wouldn't come back at all, and then what? If Gabriel didn't come back, Utuyu knew he would have to wonder what to do next all over again. And suppose Gabriel did come back and found him still squatting on his heels in the same place? What would Gabriel think? Utuyu knew what Gabriel would think. Gabriel would think he was a *really* stupid boy—too stupid to look after himself.

If I don't stay here, then that means I have to go somewhere else, Utuyu thought. He may have been only about six years old, but Utuyu already knew that "somewhere else" could mean a lot of different places. How was he supposed to choose which place to go? He didn't know where any of those lots of places were or how to get to any of them.

A voice in his head said, *Remember me,* and Utuyu remembered what the scorpion had told him. The scorpion had told him to keep his eyes open at the front of his head and his ears open at the sides, and that's when

Utuyu heard a sound unlike any sound he had heard before. Somewhere through the knees and trees in the square a band was playing. A trumpet blared out across the square, and the notes of the trumpet bounced off the walls of the buildings and flew into Utuyu's ears. His ears told him the sound was all around him at the same time. More than that, Utuyu could feel the music inside him. It had gone down to his shoulders and arms and hands, down to his hips and legs and feet. When he stuck his fingers in his ears to see what would happen, the music was still there inside him.

Wherever it's coming from, that's where I'll go, Utuyu decided, and he stood up off his heels. Keeping close to the walls of the buildings, he made his way around the sides of the square. The music got louder and louder. Then, there it was, coming from a group of men standing in front of the tables under the arches where the people were sitting. Each of the men was playing an instrument, and some of the instruments were different from the others. All the men, though, were singing at the top their voices. But the music was coming out all in one piece—except for the sounds that came from the man with the trumpet. His sounds were much louder than the rest and seemed to float away by themselves.

It was not only Utuyu's ears that were amazed. His eyes were amazed, too. The clothes on these men's knees were magnificent! The men were wearing black trousers with silver decorations all up and down the sides, all of their trousers the same. The men's jackets were the same as well, and they were black and silver, too. All the black and silver didn't stop there, though. On their heads the men were wearing enormous black-and-silver hats that reached beyond their shoulders. The only things the men were wearing that weren't black and silver were their bright, white shirts and what looked like bright, red birds perched under their chins.

Utuyu couldn't stop staring at the men. They started their music and their singing at the same time, and they stopped their music and their singing at the same time. How did they know how to do that, Utuyu wondered? Maybe it had something to do with the clothes the men were wearing, he thought. They were all dressed the same, and maybe that's why the music always came out at the same time and stopped at the same time.

Utuyu saw something else going on, something that really caught his attention. There were times when the men stopped the music, and one of them walked up to each table, and some of the people gave him coins. The people reached into their pockets and gave the man money, just like that. All the man seemed to do was smile, and out came the coins.

As Utuyu watched, he noticed that the smiling man wasn't the only person who was getting money from the people at the tables. Lots of people were getting money.

A woman with long, grey hair tied in a braid down her neck was walking around the tables. She had a basket of flowers on her head, and when she gave flowers to a person at a table, that person gave her money. It didn't happen all the time, and Utuyu wondered what made it happen when it did. He noticed that the woman didn't smile very often. The music man had smiled all the time. Maybe that was why the people didn't give the woman money as often as they gave it to the music man. The woman didn't stop at all the tables the way the music man had, either. Why did she stop at some tables and not at others, Utuyu wondered?

There were more women walking around the tables. One had a baby on her back and, under one arm, a bundle of brightly colored cloth mats. She held up the mats for the people to look at. Another woman was showing the people baskets woven out of grass. Utuyu had seen baskets like that before at Ita's house. Still another woman was holding out dolls in fancy dresses. None of the women smiled, and Utuyu thought maybe that was why the people at the tables just shook their heads and didn't reach into their pockets for money.

Three children—two girls and a boy not much bigger than Utuyu himself—were moving in and out of the tables, too. They were hardly as tall as the tables themselves. One of the girls was trying to give people bracelets woven out of different-colored threads. Most of the people at the tables shook their heads like the others, without so much as looking at the bracelets or at the girl herself. One woman at a table, though, talked to the girl, looked at all the bracelets, kept some of them, and gave the girl money—even though the girl had never smiled. In fact, this time it was the woman who gave the money who did all the smiling. That seemed strange to Utuyu, but stranger still was the woman's face. It was as white as the moon.

The second girl was trying to give the people small, flat sticks. Utuyu had no idea what the sticks were, or what they were for. Perhaps the people didn't, either, because although the girl stopped at every table, no one gave her any money, and nobody smiled. The boy was trying to give wooden combs to the people. They weren't giving him any money, either, but Utuyu wasn't surprised. The boy was frowning all the time and growled at the people when they shook their heads.

There was only one grown-up man who was trying to give things away. He was showing the people small carpets, and Utuyu could tell from the look on the man's face that he was sad. He wasn't getting any money at all from the people.

Utuyu watched carefully what was going on, but he couldn't figure it out. Where did everyone get the things they were trying to give away? Why did some of the people give them money, and others didn't? What were you supposed to do with the money, anyway, if somebody gave you some? All Utuyu could tell for sure from watching was that the people at the tables had money in their pockets, and if you had something to show them, they might give you their money, and then again, they might not. To Utuyu, walking around the tables looked easy. That was something he could do, too. And if you had nothing to show the people? What would they do then?

A man and a woman were sitting at one of the tables, talking. Utuyu walked up to them and held out his hand. "Money, please," he said.

The man and the woman went on talking as though Utuyu wasn't there. Didn't they hear him, he wondered? So he said it again, louder. "Money, please!"

The man turned to him with a frown and said something Utuyu couldn't understand at all, but he understood the man wasn't about to reach into his pocket for money. Utuyu looked at the woman and said, "Money, please?" The woman shook her head, and this time the man barked at him and waved with his hand for Utuyu to go away. Then the man and the woman went on talking.

Utuyu tried another table where three women were eating ice cream. When he asked again for money, they shook their heads, but at least they smiled. That reminded Utuyu that he should try smiling, too, so at the next table, where a man was reading a newspaper, he smiled at the man when he said, "Money, please." The man picked up his newspaper and held it up in front of his face, which Utuyu never saw again.

Not one single person gave Utuyu any money, and after a while he decided he'd have to find something to show the people—anything at all. But what? That was the problem.

Chapter Seven

Utuyu looked all around to see what there might be for him to show the people. There were stones on the ground in the bushes. Perhaps they were something he could show. On his hands and knees, Utuyu crawled about, choosing the stones he liked best because of their shapes, and filled his pockets. When his pockets could hold no more, he crawled back out of the bushes and stood up. Ooops! The stones pulled his pants right down around his ankles! Two older boys standing nearby laughed and pointed at him. Pulling his pants back up as fast as he could, Utuyu waddled over to a bench and sat down. One by one, he took the stones out of his pockets and put them in his lap. They didn't look like anything anyone would want to see. They were plain old stones, and, what's more, they were dirty.

There was a fountain close to where he was sitting. The thing to do, Utuyu decided, was to give the stones a bath. So, he made a bag for the stones out of the front of his shirt and went and sat on the edge of the fountain. There, he rubbed each stone in the water until all the dirt had come off. When he finished cleaning each one, he put it beside him on the fountain's edge. Soon, he had made a line of stones, wet and shiny, that reflected the lights around him. They looked *much* better! When he had cleaned all the stones, he put them back in his shirtfront bag and walked over to where the people were sitting.

Two things went wrong with Utuyu's plan. The first problem was that he had to hold his shirtfront with both his hands to stop the stones from falling out. This meant he had no hand left to hold out for money. The second problem was worse. When the water dried off the stones, they stopped shining under the lights and became dull. They turned back into plain old stones again—*clean* plain old stones, that's for sure, but, all the same, plain as they could be. There was nothing Utuyu could think of to do about either of these things that had gone wrong, so he went ahead and walked around all the people at the tables, showing them his clean plain old stones and hoping they would understand that they were meant to take one and give him a coin in return.

You can probably guess what happened. No one wanted one of his stones, and no one gave him any money. Disappointed, Utuyu took all his stones and dumped them in the bushes. "Go get yourselves all dirty again!" he told them. "See if I care!" Then he went back and sat on the bench again, his arms folded across his chest, feeling mad as can be.

The only good things about this place, Utuyu decided, were the balloons and the music. He would have liked to have had a balloon to hold, but he saw that you had to give the balloon seller a coin before the seller would give you one. The music, at least, was free. Other people gave the musicians money to make them play, and then everyone, everyone in the whole square, got to listen for nothing. Utuyu stayed on the bench, looking at the balloons and listening to the music. After a while, he didn't feel so mad anymore, and he began thinking again about what he could do to get the people to give him money.

In his mind, Utuyu heard the scorpion saying, *Keep your eyes open in the front of your head.*

Men were sitting on tall chairs, and other men sat in front of them, making their shoes as shiny as Utuyu's stones had been when they first came out of the fountain. When a man got out of one of the chairs, he handed over some money, and then another man got into the chair. That looked like a good way to get money, Utuyu thought. You didn't have to go to the people. They walked right over and came to you. But the men who shined the shoes had found a tall chair somewhere for the men to sit in, and they had bottles of this and that, and brushes and cloths. Utuyu, of course, had none of these things. If he'd had them, he wouldn't have known how to make someone's shoes get shiny anyway.

Utuyu looked around some more, but for a while he couldn't see anything that could be of any help. But then, from across the square, came one of Ita's children. His name was Nino, and he had a tray in front of him, with a strap that went up around his neck to help hold it up. On the tray were little packets of things to eat, gum to chew, cigarettes to smoke, and bottles of things to drink. Utuyu had seen boys and girls with these kinds of trays before. Now and then people would take something from the children's trays and give them money.

"Nino!" Utuyu shouted. Nino waved back, and the two of them went to sit together on an empty bench.

"How's it going?" Nino asked.

"Sort of okay, I guess," Utuyu said. He told Nino about Gabriel, and how Gabriel had stopped him from getting squashed on the street and showed him the way to the square with the balloons. "But I don't know what I'm supposed to do now," he said.

"You do whatever comes next," Nino said. "Something always comes next."

"Where am I supposed to sleep?" Utuyu asked, and as soon as he said it, he realized that sleeping was what he really wanted to do most. He was tired, tired and sleepy.

"You can sleep anywhere you want," Nino said. "Anywhere, that is, where people can't see you, or they'll chase you away."

"Where are you going to sleep? Can I sleep there, too?" Utuyu asked.

"No way!" Nino said. "When I come to the city, I go to a secret place where some other kids sleep, too. They'd be really mad at me if I brought someone else there. You're gonna have to find your own place."

"And how can I find something to show the people so they'll give me money?" Utuyu asked. "Like, where did you get all that stuff on your tray?"

"It's not my stuff," Nino said. "It belongs to a friend of mine who's sick, so I got his tray tonight."

"Where does *he* get all the stuff?" Utuyu asked.

"He's got a mother, and she buys it for him," explained Nino. "Then she sends him out here to get more money from the people than she paid for the stuff. He's lucky like that to have a mother."

"And when you don't have the tray?" Utuyu asked. "How do you get money then?"

"Oh, I've got ways," Nino said. "I go to a big grocery store and they let me put the stuff people buy in bags. Some of the people give me money."

"What's a grocery store?" Utuyu asked.

Nino told him it was a place people could buy food and lots of other things, too. "But you're still too little for the people to let you work there," Nino said.

What Nino was saying wasn't any help at all. "So what am I supposed to do?" Utuyu said.

"You'll find something," Nino said. "There's a ton of people here in the city, and there's lots of money. All you've gotta do is think up a way to get ahold of it. That's what we're all doing." Then Nino said, "I gotta go and get ahold of some more of it right now, or I won't get this tray again. 'Bye, Utuyu, see you around."

When Nino left, Utuyu stayed on the bench. *Keep your ears open on the sides of your head,* said the scorpion in Utuyu's mind.

My ears ARE open! Utuyu thought. *And I'm too tired to open them any wider. All I can hear is the music!*

Keep your tongue closed in your mouth, the scorpion seemed to say, *like a bird in a cage.*

That's when Utuyu got an idea. The musicians didn't have anything, not one single thing, to *show* anybody. They just made music. *I can make music, too,* Utuyu said to himself. *My tongue can sing, just like a bird in its cage.* All at once he didn't feel so tired anymore.

Utuyu went to a table where four people were talking. There were two men and two women. One of the men and one of the women were mad at each other. They were frowning and held their shoulders up around their ears. Their voices were loud and unpleasant. The other man and the other woman were trying to stop the other two shouting. Not one of the four of them looked at Utuyu when he came near their table, but when he was standing right *at* their table, and put his hands *on* their table, they all stopped talking for a moment and looked at him. Now, all four of them looked mad. One of the men shook his head. The other man waved for Utuyu to go away. Then they all went back to talking and shouting at each other.

Utuyu didn't move. He stood right there with his hands on the people's table and began to sing. He sang a song about a bird that Ita had sung to him many times. It was a favorite song of the people who came to stay for a while at Ita's house.

The words of songs in Utuyu's language don't rhyme the way they usually do in our language. That is, the different words at the end of the lines don't sound alike, the way "wing" and "sing" sound alike in what I'm going to write for you. I just thought you might like it better this way. And my words aren't exactly the same as the ones in Utuyu's song, either. I think, though, that what's important in a song is what it says.

This is what Utuyu's song said:

A bird in a bush with a broken wing
Opened her beak and began to sing.
"I'm small and frail and made to fly,
But boys throw stones, and I don't know why."

A boy walking by held out his arm.
"Come, and I'll keep you safe from harm.
I'll care for your wing 'til it's healed, and then
I'll set you free to fly again."

He cradled the bird against his chest.
"Why are you kinder than all the rest?"
Asked the bird. Said the boy, "Because, like you,
Boys throw stones at me, too."

At first the angry people went on talking and shouting as if Utuyu wasn't there. Then they stopped talking and shouting and frowned at him. They didn't know Utuyu's language, and so they couldn't understand the words of his song. But then Utuyu's sweet voice stopped them frowning, and their faces became kinder. Utuyu's song was only a little song. It didn't last very long. He was afraid the people would go back to talking and shouting, so when he'd finished his song the first time, he began it again. The people listened. The angry man and the angry woman let their shoulders go back down to where they belonged, and the other man put his arm around the other woman.

They listened until Utuyu had finished singing his song a second time. Then both men reached into their pockets, and both women opened their purses, and all four of them gave him coins. Utuyu couldn't help smiling, and the four people smiled back. One of the women reached out and patted him on the cheek. Utuyu put the coins in his pocket, and when he left them to go to another table, the four people were still smiling and talking to each other in quiet voices.

The people at the next table he went to gave him money, too. A little distance away, there was a big table with lots of people sitting around it, and they all had faces as pale white as the moon. One of them waved at Utuyu for him to come over and sing to them, and when he did, they gestured for him to sing again, and then they clapped their hands and all gave him coins. Utuyu could feel his pockets getting a little heavy again, not so heavy that they were about to fall down around his ankles, but he could feel there was something in them, and that was a good feeling.

What felt empty now, instead of his pockets, was his stomach. The next time he sang to a table of people, he pointed to the food they were eating, and one of the people gave him a big piece of flat bread like the bread Ita was always making. On the bread were pieces of cheese and avocado and tomato and chicken. Another gave him a whole handful of tiny, fried grasshoppers. (You may never have thought of eating grasshoppers, but in Oaxaca, people like them a lot and eat them like peanuts.) There was no way Utuyu could eat and sing at the same time, and he wanted to eat much more than he wanted to sing right then, so he went and sat on a bench and ate the food the people had given him. He ate the grasshoppers in one, big mouthful, and then he ate the bread with everything on it. He didn't just eat it, he gobbled it all up.

Utuyu's stomach felt so good to have food in it after such a long, empty day, that it burped. He patted his stomach, and then he patted his pockets to make sure the money was still there, and then he yawned. It had been a *very* long day, a day that had started so long ago high up in The Mountains to the North at Ita's house and was ending now in the city of Oaxaca. He looked at all the buildings around him, at the tall lights up on sticks, at the people walking around and around, and still the music was coming from somewhere over beyond the trees . . . and the music was the last thing he remembered before being shaken awake by a man in a uniform, who was clearly telling him to get off the bench and go away. Utuyu had forgotten what Nino had said about sleeping somewhere where no one could see you.

Chapter Eight

For a moment, Utuyu didn't know where he was. Everything around him had changed. There weren't so many lights, and the buildings were just dark shapes around the edges of the square. There were hardly any people, and the music had stopped. No one was selling anything anymore. The only balloons he could see were in one big bunch that a woman was carrying, and she and her balloons were about to disappear out of sight around a corner. Utuyu had no idea where to go, so he ran after the balloons to see where they were going. He followed the balloon woman as she walked through the streets of the dark city until she suddenly stopped at an enormous metal door. She reached into her pocket and took out a key. That's when she saw Utuyu standing behind her.

"What do *you* want?" she said, and for once Utuyu could understand what someone was saying. The woman talked the same way he talked.

Utuyu was so surprised that he didn't know what to answer. He stood there and looked at the woman holding her balloons.

"What's the matter? Can't you talk?" the woman said.

Utuyu said the first thing that came into his head. "I want a balloon," he said.

The woman laughed. "*You* can't pay for a balloon!" she said and opened the big door.

"I can, too!" Utuyu said and took some of the coins from his pocket.

"Well, well, how about that?" said the woman. "So where did you get all that money? Did you steal it or something?"

"I didn't steal it," said Utuyu. "I sang, and the people gave it to me."

The woman looked at him closely in the light that was coming from the open door. "*You're* not the one who was singing," she said. "We all saw that boy. He was much bigger than you."

"I am, too!" said Utuyu.

"Then sing," said the woman.

So Utuyu sang his song about the bird again, and the woman smiled.

"So it *was* you," she said. "Okay then, which balloon do you want?"

There were so many balloons that Utuyu didn't know which one to choose.

"Hurry up now," said the woman. "I'm not going to stand here all night!"

Utuyu pointed to a yellow balloon that was in the shape of a dog. The woman untied it from the bunch and handed it to him. Utuyu held out his coins, but the woman didn't take one. "I didn't pay you for your song, so you don't have to pay me for my balloon," she said. Then she said, "Come here," and tied the balloon to Utuyu's wrist.

"How about I sleep in there tonight," Utuyu said, pointing with his other hand to the open door.

The woman shook her head. "Are you crazy? There are so many of us in there already that there's no room for even a little sprout like you!" She finished tying the balloon to Utuyu's wrist and said, "Now off you go!" Then she went into the building with her balloons and shut the big door with a clang that echoed down the dark street.

The street was *very* dark. Utuyu walked a little way along it, wondering what he should do now, and then he heard the sound of someone snoring. He followed the sound to a deep doorway, and there was a man all curled up in the doorway, sleeping, but he wasn't alone. Tucked up against him was a boy smaller than Utuyu himself. The boy was sleeping, too.

This time, Utuyu remembered what Nino had said about sleeping where no one could see you, but he was too tired and sleepy to care. If the man and the boy could sleep there in the doorway, then he'd go ahead and sleep there as well. Very, very carefully, Utuyu crawled into the doorway. More carefully still, he laid his head on the man's arm and snuggled up against the boy. Nobody awoke.

Utuyu made sure his yellow-dog balloon was still tied to his wrist, and it was. The balloon, itself, rested safely up against the top of the doorway, like a yellow-dog moon. Utuyu snuggled in a little closer to the man and the boy, and then he fell asleep.

Chapter Nine

The sun came up over the top of the building opposite where Utuyu was sleeping and flooded his doorway with sudden warmth and light. That wasn't what woke him up, though. What woke him up was a great sound that filled the sky. It was as if the sun were a gong, and someone had hit it with a huge, heavy hammer. Whoever it was up there didn't hit the gong just once, but went on hitting it again and again and again until Utuyu was wide-awake.

The first thing he noticed was that he was alone in the doorway. The man was gone, and the boy, too. The second thing he noticed was that his balloon had gone as well. All that was left of it was the string around his wrist. Worse than that, when he put his hand in his pocket, he found almost all his coins were gone. There were only three left. If it hadn't been for the string on his wrist and those three coins, Utuyu might have thought that the musicians, and the people at the tables, and the great bunches of balloons themselves, had all been a dream.

Utuyu sat there, his back up against one side of the doorway, his arms around his knees and a big scowl on his face.

"So, Sky Boy, did you get a good night's sleep?" said a voice behind him.

Utuyu turned, and there was Gabriel looking down at him. Utuyu turned his back without answering.

"Woke up in a bad mood, huh?" said Gabriel.

Utuyu still didn't answer and went on scowling.

"I watched you last night," said Gabriel. "You were doing pretty well with the people at the tables. You figured things out real fast."

Utuyu felt a little bit better, but he still didn't say anything.

"How much money did you get?" Gabriel asked.

"I don't know," Utuyu said.

"Show me, and I'll tell you," said Gabriel.

Utuyu reached into his pocket and showed Gabriel the three coins.

"Hey, you did better than that," said Gabriel. "I saw you."

"Somebody took the rest. While I was sleeping. And took my balloon, too," said Utuyu. Once again he felt that if he didn't try hard not to, he was going to cry whether he wanted to or not.

Gabriel shook his head. "You've still got a whole lot to learn," he said. "Everyone's looking for money around here. Money and food. When you get some stuff to eat, you eat it right away. You don't leave it lying around. And when you find a way to get some money, you hold on to it. You don't leave it loose in your pocket and then go to sleep! If you do, then it's somebody else's good luck."

"So what was I supposed to do with it?" said Utuyu. "Nobody can stay awake all the time!"

"If you don't do anything else, you can at least twist the bottom of your pockets around the money. Then somebody will think your pocket's empty when they reach in, or if they don't, they'll really have to wake you up to get at the money." Gabriel pulled one of his pockets inside out and showed Utuyu how to twist the bottom into a tight little bag of its own.

"Where did you sleep?" Utuyu asked Gabriel.

"At Father Juan's place. With the other kids."

"Where's that?" asked Utuyu.

"Not far," said Gabriel.

"Can I sleep there, too?" asked Utuyu.

"No," said Gabriel. "There's already too many kids there. Besides, you only get to sleep there if you turn up at his school."

"What's 'school'?" asked Utuyu. It was a word he'd never heard before.

"It's a place kids go to learn things. That's how I learned to speak the way all the people speak here. You can't understand anything they say, can you?"

Utuyu shook his head.

"See? That's what I mean."

Utuyu thought about that. "Where is he, anyway?"

"Father Juan? He's working. This is his busy day. It's Sunday, and Sunday is always his busy day."

"What does he do?" asked Utuyu.

"He runs the church," said Gabriel.

"Church" was another word Utuyu hadn't heard before, so he asked Gabriel what it meant, too.

"It's a place lots of people go, especially on Sunday," said Gabriel. "They all sing and say things, and Father Juan talks to them. You want to see how it works?"

Utuyu nodded his head.

"Okay," said Gabriel. "Follow me."

Utuyu followed Gabriel back the way he had come the night before. Utuyu recognized the door where the woman had gone with her balloons. The door was shut. They came to the big square, but it didn't look anything like Utuyu remembered. There was hardly anyone walking around, and where all the people had been sitting, men and women in white shirts and black pants and skirts were sweeping the ground and wiping the empty tables. As he and Gabriel were crossing the square, the big sound in the sky began again. Gabriel pointed up to the top of the largest building of all the buildings around the square. Where Gabriel was pointing, Utuyu could see a bell swinging back and forth, and he could tell that was where the sound in the sky was coming from.

"That means it's a church," said Gabriel. "And that's a big one! Maybe the biggest in all of Oaxaca. But it's not the one where Father Juan works."

They went on through the streets for a while. There weren't so many cars and trucks and busses as there had been the day before, but Utuyu still watched carefully when they crossed from one side of a street to the other. He hadn't forgotten his banana that got squashed.

Gabriel stopped in front of a building that had carvings of stone people around the door. There were lots of real people going inside, and the door was so big that it made the grownups going in look small. Music was coming from the inside of the building, but it was a very different kind of music from the music the musicians had been making in the square. Instead of making Utuyu feel happy, it made him feel scared, as though something terrible was about to happen.

"Come on," said Gabriel, going through the door. Utuyu shook his head.

"What's the matter with you?" said Gabriel.

"I don't want to go in," said Utuyu. "It smells funny in there."

"I though you said you wanted to see how it worked," said Gabriel.

"I can see from here," said Utuyu, and he stayed right by the door.

It looked to Utuyu that there was only one room in the building, but that room was enormous. It went way up over his head—so far that although there were pictures on the ceiling, Utuyu couldn't see what they were. The walls were all white, and there were pictures on the walls, too. Utuyu didn't like those pictures at all. Everyone in the pictures looked sad, and in several of the pictures he could see that a man was being hurt by other men. Far away at the end of the room there was a statue of a woman in a glass box. All Utuyu could see of the woman was the whiteness of her face. Her face was as white as some of those strange faces he saw in the square. The statue was covered in a big blue dress with shiny things on it that went up around the woman's head. Because the statue was so far away, Utuyu couldn't tell if the woman looked happy or sad.

A man came out from somewhere and stood in front of the statue.

"That's Father Juan," Gabriel said.

The man had wavy, black hair on his head that came down around his ears and turned into a short, black beard. A voice that filled the room said something to all the people who were sitting on rows of benches, and they all bent forward on their knees. The voice went on speaking the language Utuyu couldn't understand, and suddenly all the people stood up. It looked to Utuyu like the voice was giving the people orders, and they were doing what it told them to do. It was like being in Ita's house. You did what you were told.

"Where's that voice coming from?" Utuyu asked Gabriel.

"That's Father Juan's voice," said Gabriel. "He talks into a thing called a microphone that makes his voice louder so that everyone can hear him."

Father Juan must have told the people to start singing, because all at once that's what everyone started doing. Utuyu didn't like the song the people were singing at all. It was slow, and like everything else in this place, it made him feel sad and worried. He liked his own songs much better. Utuyu looked around the room once more. There was nothing in it that made him feel happy, and he could see that not a single person of all the people who were there felt happy, either. He looked at Father Juan, who was still talking. He couldn't see if Father Juan looked happy, but his loud voice didn't sound like it. Utuyu wasn't sure that he wanted to meet Father Juan after all.

Chapter Ten

Have you ever felt you didn't want to go into a strange place where there were lots of strange people you didn't know? I know I have. When that happens, we may need to take our time to think about how we feel and not let people push us faster than we're ready to go. That's why Utuyu stayed at the door of the church, watching, even though Gabriel kept telling him they should go inside.

"I don't want to go in there," he told Gabriel each time Gabriel said they should.

"You're a funny kid," said Gabriel.

The more Utuyu watched what was going on inside the church, the less he liked the look of it all.

"I want to go," he said.

"We just got here!" said Gabriel.

"I want to go," Utuyu said again. "I want to go away."

"Then go, Sky Boy," said Gabriel. "I'm going to stay for a while."

"Let's go find something to eat," said Utuyu. "I'm hungry."

"If you stay 'til Father Juan's done, he might give us something to eat," said Gabriel.

But although Utuyu was hungry, he wasn't hungry enough to want to stay in that sad place anymore. "I'm going," he said.

"'Bye, then, Sky Boy," said Gabriel. "And try to be smart this time. Know what I mean?"

Utuyu went back into the streets. He wasn't sure where he was. He thought he knew, more or less, the way back to the big square, but after wandering about for half an hour, he hadn't found it. On one of his many turns this way and that way, he came across a woman who had a lot of different kinds of bread out on a tray. She had the same kind of face as Ita's people had. In fact, she looked a little bit like Ita, herself. Utuyu went up to her and held out his three coins.

"You can't get much with that," said the woman in Utuyu's language.

"I don't have any more," said Utuyu.

"Where are you from?" the woman asked.

"Up in the mountains," said Utuyu.

"I can tell that!" said the woman. "Where in the mountains?"

"I don't know," said Utuyu. "Ita's house."

"That doesn't tell me anything," said the woman. "How long have you been in the city?"

"I came yesterday," Utuyu told the woman. "In a truck."

The woman shook her head. "How old are you, anyway?"

Utuyu shrugged.

"How do you think you're going to stay alive around here?"

"I can sing," said Utuyu.

"What can you sing?" asked the woman.

Utuyu began singing his bird song for her. Right after he began, the woman began singing along with him. She knew the song, too.

"What other songs do you know?" the woman asked when they were done singing.

"I know lots more songs," said Utuyu. "As many as can be."

The woman laughed. "That's good," she said, "because you're going to need them if you're going to stay alive by singing." Then she said, "Sit," and gave Utuyu a roll with sugar on the outside and jam on the inside. Utuyu held out his coins again, but the woman shook her head. "Keep your money. You have a sweet voice, and you can stay right here and sing all your songs. We'll see if anyone comes to listen and buy my bread."

So that's what Utuyu did. He stayed with the woman, and when he sang to the people passing by, several of them stopped to listen, and some of the several who stopped bought the woman's bread. By the time it was growing dark, she had sold a lot of bread. "Time for me to go home," she said. "My children will be hungry." Utuyu hoped the woman would say that he could go home with her, but she didn't. What she did do, though, was take some of her money and buy Utuyu a big piece of flat bread with meat and cheese and sauce on it—that, and a large paper cup of fruit water.

"There," she said, packing up the rest of her bread. "That should help you sing. I'm here every Sunday. You can come by whenever you want and sing to the people. If I sell more bread because of your singing, I'll buy you something to eat." Then she put what was left of her bread in a basket and balanced the basket on the top of her head.

"Where's the big place with the balloons?" Utuyu asked her.

The woman pointed, and at that very moment the same sound of the bell from the big church filled the sky again. "Keep walking toward the bell, and after a while you'll see the church it's coming from. That's where the balloons are," the woman said, and then she walked off down the street.

That night, Utuyu sang his songs to the people sitting at the tables around the square. By the time he was too tired to sing anymore, he had lots of coins in his pocket once again. Two people had given him part of the food they were eating, and his stomach was quiet and content.

Utuyu didn't go back to the same doorway where he'd slept before. He walked in a different direction this time, looking for a place that was further away from people. When he came to a small park that was dark and empty, he decided that was where he would sleep. There were bushes in the park, and Utuyu went to the furthest-away bushes and crept underneath. If people passed by, they wouldn't be able to see him.

Before he fell asleep, he remembered to twist his money into a tight little bag at the bottom of his pocket.

Chapter Eleven

U tuyu's life began to take on a shape. That is, little by little, there began to be some things that Utuyu did every day at about the same time. Utuyu didn't know how to tell time, of course, but that didn't matter. Days have a shape of their own, whether anyone is telling time or not. That's so, no matter where we are in this world.

In Oaxaca, like everywhere else, the morning begins when the sky gets bright. Then the sun comes up over the mountains, and then over the buildings of the city, and the day gets warmer. By the time the sun is right above your head, and you have to look straight up to see it, the day is hot. Slowly, the sun moves further and further away from the mountains where it began, away from being right above you, and gets lower down in the other side of the sky. As the sun gets lower and lower, the air gets cooler again, and the light is not as bright as it was. By the time you can't see the sun anymore, because it has disappeared behind the buildings and the mountains beyond them, the day has become cooler still—much cooler and much darker. Then the day gets dark altogether. It stops being day and turns into night. It stays night for a long time, and then night begins being day again, just the way it did before.

There were other ways, too, that Utuyu could tell his own kind of time. There were the loud church bells that always began ringing when the day was getting light, and then rang at other times, too, but always when the sun seemed to be in the same place. There were times when the streets were empty, when there were hardly any people, or cars, or busses, or trucks moving around at all. Then there were other times when the streets became so busy and full that Utuyu felt better staying still in one place and not getting in the way of everything that was going on. These were good times to watch what people did, to listen to the voice of the scorpion in his mind and keep his eyes open in front of his head.

The big square with the balloons was the best place to watch what people were doing, and the comings and the goings of the people there were another way for Utuyu to tell time. There were times, like the early morning, when no one was sitting at the tables, when there were only the men and women in white shirts and black pants and skirts sweeping the ground, wiping the tables, and covering them with purple and yellow and blue cloths.

Soon, though, people would come from the streets around the square and sit at the tables, and from then on, as the day became hotter and the sun moved up overhead, there would be more and more people in the square, but only for a while. Many of them went away as the sun got lower in the sky and the day became cooler, but then they all seemed to come back again as the day grew darker. By the time the lights came on around the square, there were more people there than ever. That was when the most women and men and children walked about the square with things to show the people. That was the time when the men shining people's shoes in the tall chairs were busiest, too.

If the day had not had a shape of its own, and if the church bells had not been ringing and the people coming and going, Utuyu would still have known what time it was. For instance, his stomach told him when it was time to eat, and his head told him when it was time to sleep. When his stomach and his head told him these things, Utuyu listened. If he didn't, he knew he would soon start feeling a certain kind of awful—an awful that could hurt and make him dizzy.

Keeping his stomach quiet and his head happy took up a lot of Utuyu's time. During the day, it was his stomach that complained to him the loudest and kept him busy searching for food. It was only after it had been dark for a long time, after he had been singing to the people at the tables in the square, that his head began to spin. Utuyu knew his head was telling him it was time to find his way back to the bushes in the small park, time to crawl under the bushes where no one could see him. His head was telling him it was time to sleep during the long night, to go to sleep until the day began once more.

Utuyu learned to get along with the things his stomach and mind were telling him every day—except for one thing. He didn't like it when his stomach told him the time by telling him it was time to let stuff out. That's something everyone has to do, because otherwise a stomach wouldn't have any more room to put more food in, would it? It would get so full it couldn't hold any more. Utuyu didn't mind when it was only water he had to let out. He could do that almost anywhere, and people didn't seem to mind. But when Utuyu's stomach began growling in his backside, then it became a real problem.

At Ita's house, there was a place everyone went to let stuff out, but where was he supposed to go for that with all the buildings and people around him? For the first day or two in Oaxaca, Utuyu had tried not to listen to his stomach growling in his backside, but after a while, his stomach made such a fuss about it that Utuyu had to squat down right where he was and let stuff out, right there between two parked cars on a street full of people walking by.

It only took a moment for Utuyu to learn that that's not what people do in the city! The people walking by made nasty, ugly faces at him. A man came out of a doorway and shouted. Another man in a uniform came all the way from the street corner and shouted at him more loudly still. Utuyu didn't like having everyone passing by looking at him and shouting at him, but the whole city of Oaxaca could have stared and shouted. Utuyu would have had to go on doing what he was doing until his stomach let him stop. That's the way stomachs are.

That was a bad situation. The only thing that kept it from being worse was that no one seemed to want to touch him. If they had, Utuyu felt sure the people would have given him a beating. When his stomach finally quit complaining, Utuyu yanked up his pants and ran for his life.

After that, Utuyu tried to make his stomach wait until it was dark and he could find a place where no one could see him. That solved Utuyu's big problem, but there was still a small one. In the place people went at Ita's house, there were always pieces of paper you could use to clean your backside after your stomach had finished growling. That small problem was easy to solve, though. There was paper everywhere in the city. All Utuyu had to remember was to grab some when he saw it—in trash cans, under tables, or blowing in the street—and to remember to always keep some paper in his pocket.

After Utuyu had been in the city for something like a week, he made a discovery that made his life a lot easier. Near the park where he slept, he saw a place where the buildings seemed to have fallen down a long time ago. There were boards around it that were supposed to keep people out, but whoever had put up the boards hadn't been thinking about keeping out someone as small as Utuyu. Here and there the boards were just far enough apart for him to squeeze through.

The first time he dared to squeeze himself between the boards, he did it because he had to. His backside suddenly started growling in the middle of the day, growling the way he didn't like, and Utuyu could tell his backside wasn't about to wait until nighttime. That first time, he didn't stay in the place behind the boards any longer than he had to. There were pieces of buildings tumbled all over each other, piled much too high for him to see over. There were bushes and some small trees, sprouting wherever they could, and Utuyu couldn't see what was behind them. All he could see was that it was a long way to the next tall building the far side of the place, and who could tell what there might be in between? That first time he squeezed through the boards, he didn't feel ready to find out.

That night, asleep underneath the bushes in his park, with new coins from his singing twisted into the bottom of one pocket and paper stuffed into the other, Utuyu dreamed about the place behind the boards. It was dark there, but he could see everything just fine. That didn't seem strange to Utuyu, because he wasn't awake to think it was strange. If he'd been awake, he wouldn't have been wherever it is that dreams appear, where everything is strange and anything can happen—a place where, no matter if it's dark, you can see everything around you.

In his dream, he was looking down from a high place, and he could see Ita's children running around the piles of what was left of the old buildings. They seemed to be looking for something under the bushes and trees. Because it was his dream, no one had to tell Utuyu what Ita's children were looking for. They were looking for him. Ita was there, too, inside a room in one of the ruined buildings. In his dream, Utuyu could see through the walls of the small room, and there was Ita, feeding flat bread to the scorpion. They were talking, and Utuyu could hear what they were saying.

"The bells don't stop ringing," Ita said.
"They're hungry," said the scorpion.
"And dirty!" said Ita.

Then, in the dream, Ita's children started calling. Utuyu could see them below him, still chasing around through the bushes. Utuyu opened his mouth and began to sing. The children looked up . . . and the dream ended.

Chapter Twelve

When Utuyu awoke from his dream, the sky was already light, but the streets around him were quieter than usual. The loud church bells rang as they always did, but their sound bounced through the streets that were almost empty of people.

Utuyu remembered his dream clearly. In his mind, he was still seeing the place with the fallen-down buildings just the way he'd seen it in his dream—looking down on it all from a high place. He could see Ita's children running around looking for him, and he wondered if somewhere in that place, the real place not the dream place, there was a room, like the one he'd seen in his dream where Ita had been talking to the scorpion.

The sun had already come up over the mountains, and now it rose up above the buildings and filled Utuyu's park with its warmth. He sat there beneath the bushes, thinking about the place he'd dreamed about. The more he thought about his dream and the place behind the boards, the more he wondered what the rest of that place was like. His wondering about it didn't help him at all. It only made him more curious to find out, and his curiosity made him wonder more. There's only so much wondering about something that a person can do without wanting to find out about that something for real. By the time the sun was a little higher, that was how much wondering Utuyu had done. He made up his mind to go to the place and see for himself.

The street outside the boards was quiet. The doors of the houses were all shut, and only one person and one car and one bus passed as Utuyu looked for the space between the boards where he could squeeze through. Behind the boards, it was quieter still. The sun was hot now. The piles of stones and rocks and pieces of old buildings lay there, not moving, not making a sound. They looked like they had been lying there forever, just the way they were. Not even the air moved. The bushes and small trees were as still as the rocks. The only thing that moved in that place behind the boards was Utuyu himself, and he moved very slowly.

Beyond the first pile of fallen-down buildings was another. Beyond the second one was another . . . and then another and another after that. Utuyu felt like he was walking between hills of stone, and in some places he had to crawl on all fours over the lower hills that blocked his way. The sun's heat was in the stones now. They were warm when Utuyu touched them. The heat seemed to be coming from everywhere around him, from the ground upwards, and from side to side, and of course the most heat poured down on him from the sun above his head. Only the small trees gave any shade. Utuyu stopped and sat under one of them. All he could see around him were hills of stone, and one hill looked much the same as another. He wondered if he would ever find his way back to the space he'd squeezed through between the boards.

Utuyu remembered that in his dream he had been somewhere up high and able to see all around. *So that's what I'll do,* he thought. *I'll climb up to the top of one of the hills and see what I can see from up there.* Carefully, on all fours, he crept up the side of the highest of the hills around him. Some of the stones slipped when he grabbed onto them, and others were sharp on his knees, but little by little,

Utuyu made it to the top of the hill. From up there, he felt like he was looking at a different world altogether.

Looking in the direction from which he'd come, he could see a yellow building. There was a dog on the roof of the yellow building, walking back and forth along the edge of the roof, stopping now and then to stare down into the street. Suddenly the dog stopped his walking back and forth, stared right at Utuyu, and started barking.

Looking in the other direction, the direction he'd been going, Utuyu could see a green building, and on the roof of the green building clothes were hanging out on a line to dry—blue pants, shirts that were purple and red and orange, and big squares of white sheets.

Now I can find my way, Utuyu thought. *If I want to go back to the hole in the boards, I'll look for the yellow building, or maybe the dog will bark and tell me which way it is. If I want to keep going ahead, I'll look for the green building with the clothes hanging on top of it.*

Utuyu knew that the green building wouldn't always have all the colors hanging out on the roof. When the washing was dry, someone would take it away, just as Ita always did up in The Mountains to the North, but he felt sure that the building would stay green.

From up high where he was, Utuyu could now see over and around the hills of stone below him. A little distance toward the green building, he could see that there was a flat space between the hills. It didn't look very big, certainly not as big as the cleared space in front of Ita's house where she made the flat bread, but it looked plenty big enough to walk around in without having to climb over anything. Utuyu had had enough of climbing over everything to get anywhere, so he crawled backwards down the side of the hill he'd climbed up and made his way between the hills, in the direction of the green building, toward the flat space he'd seen. Behind him, the dog on the roof of the yellow building was still barking.

When he got to the flat space, Utuyu found that it was bigger than it had looked from up high. If he'd felt like it, he could have run around in it, but it was much too hot to do any running around. In fact, the flat space between the hills was hotter than anywhere else so far. It was so hot that Utuyu looked for a place where he could get out of the sun, and there, in a corner of the flat space he hadn't been able to see from up high, was what was left of a room of one of the buildings that had fallen down.

Three walls of the room were still standing with window openings in two of the walls, but the best part was that most of the ceiling of the room was still there. Utuyu went into the room, out of the sun. Right away, the air around him became much cooler. He could tell someone had been in the room before. There were some old plastic bags in one corner. In the middle of the room, there was a black place on the ground with some pieces of burnt wood lying on it. Someone had once made a fire there.

Utuyu sat down on the ground, against one of the cool walls, and decided this was a fine place to be. It wasn't quite like the room in his dream where Ita had been talking to the scorpion, but it was something like it. He thought about his place under the bushes in the park and how he had to hide from the people walking by. Here in the room, he didn't have to hide from anyone, because there was no one to hide from. If his backside started growling, there were plenty of places in the rocky hills outside where he could go, and there would be no one to stare and shout at him.

Yes, he thought, *this is a fine place. I will stay here, and no one will know where I am.*

His next thought didn't come from his head. It came from his stomach. His stomach was telling time again. It was telling him it was time to find something to eat. Utuyu would have liked to have stayed right where he was until the day got cooler, but he knew he'd better listen to what his stomach was telling him. If he didn't, he'd start feeling that kind of awful again. And when the day got cooler and darker, he wanted to go back to the place with the balloons and sing some more and try to get some more coins. Singing was harder when his stomach was talking to him at the same time.

Utuyu felt his pockets. One had paper in it, and one had the coins people had already given him. The pocket with the coins in it was getting heavy. There were almost too many coins in it now to twist into a bag at the bottom of that pocket when he went to sleep.

I don't have to take the coins with me everywhere now, he thought. *I can hide them somewhere here where nobody can find them.*

Utuyu took one of the old plastic bags in the corner of the room, and into it he emptied his coin pocket. Then he took the bag outside and found a place in the stones of one of the hills where he could hide it. The stone he hid the bag under was whiter than the rest, so he knew he would be able to find the bag again when he wanted to.

I don't have to carry around all this paper, Utuyu thought. *Just a little bit. I can leave the rest in the room for when I need it.*

That's what he did. He kept enough paper in his pocket for just in case, and the rest he stuffed into a broken part of one of the walls of the room. His pockets were almost empty now, but he knew where everything was.

"Food!" his stomach said, and it didn't say it nicely. Utuyu walked out of his new home, into the flat place outside the room and into the hot, bright sun. He knew, more or less, which way the yellow building was, and that's the way he went, climbing back over the low parts of the hills.

If you'd been a bird in the sky once again, you would have seen Utuyu way down below looking like a little brown animal crawling up and down through the stony, grey hills. You'd have seen, too, that the little brown animal that was Utuyu wasn't going quite in the right direction to get to the yellow building. More or less, but not quite. From up in the sky, you'd have heard the dog on the roof of the yellow building start barking again, and you'd have seen the little brown animal that was Utuyu change the way he was going through the hills and head for the sound of the barking dog.

When Utuyu came to the boards along the street, he was in the right place. The hole he'd squeezed through to get in was right nearby, and he squeezed back through it to get out. The street was still quiet. The doors of all the houses were still shut. But as soon as Utuyu appeared through the boards into the street, the dog on the roof of the yellow building in front of him stared at him and started barking more loudly than ever. The dog was a big dog, brown with a white tail and a face that was mostly white as well. The dog's face was fierce looking. Utuyu could see his long teeth when he barked. But his white tail was wagging back and forth as fast as it could go.

Utuyu looked up at the dog, and the dog looked down at Utuyu, barking all the time. Utuyu didn't feel afraid of the dog. To begin with, the dog was way up there on the roof, and Utuyu was way down there in the street. More than that, though, there was something about the way the dog was barking and wagging its tail at the same time that told Utuyu the dog wasn't really mad at all. It was more like he was barking because he wanted to come down in the street and find out what Utuyu smelled like.

A voice in the yellow house shouted something, and the dog stopped barking and whined instead.

Utuyu called up to the roof. "Thank you for getting me to the right place," he shouted.

The dog wagged his tail and then disappeared into the building.

Chapter Thirteen

U tuyu walked through the quiet streets toward the place with the balloons. There was always food there, and he felt sure that with a song or two, he would get something to eat. Here and there houses and shops were beginning to wake up. A woman was sweeping the sidewalk in front of one house, and as he passed another, somebody threw a bucket of water out the door. Utuyu jumped out of the way—and just in time.

A man on a bicycle came pedaling down the street. He pedaled up to Utuyu and got off his bicycle right in front of him. Utuyu thought the man was going to tell him something, but he didn't. Instead, the man leaned his bicycle up against the building and took some keys out of his pocket. He bent down to unfasten something at the bottom of what looked like a grey, metal wall. Utuyu stopped to see what the man was doing. With a big heave, the man raised up the metal wall, and there behind it was a large glass window. Behind the window were lots of things on shelves. Some of the things Utuyu had seen before. There were sheets of paper of different colors, pens and pencils, books with brightly colored pictures on the front. There were also many things Utuyu had never seen before, and so he went up to the window to get a better look.

The man smiled at Utuyu, pointed at the window, and said something Utuyu didn't understand. The man squatted down on his heels next to Utuyu and said it again. Then the man's face changed. He stopped smiling and stood up, frowning. He looked down at Utuyu and said something different, and whatever he said this time, it wasn't friendly. He shook his head and waved Utuyu away with the back of his hand. Then he unlocked a door next to the window and went inside. Through the window, Utuyu could see the man turning on the lights and moving things around.

When Utuyu got to the big square, it was still quiet there, too. There weren't any balloons. The men and women wearing white and black had already put their colored tablecloths on the tables, but hardly anyone was sitting at the tables. The men were standing around, talking to each other, looking as if they were waiting for something to happen, but nothing did.

One of the men waved at Utuyu like he'd seen him before. Utuyu didn't remember seeing the man before, but he waved back anyway and walked over toward where the man was talking to his friends. The man pointed at Utuyu, said something to the other men, and they all nodded and smiled. Utuyu stopped a little distance away and looked at them. The man who had waved motioned for Utuyu to come on over, closer. Utuyu did, and then the man asked him a question. Utuyu could tell it was a question, but he had no idea what the question was.

What the man had said in the language Utuyu didn't understand was, "You're the kid who sings, right?"

Good smells were coming from the place where the men were standing, and Utuyu's stomach started complaining again, complaining loudly. Utuyu hoped maybe the man had asked him if he was hungry, so he nodded in answer to the man's question. It looked to Utuyu like it was the wrong answer. In fact, it had been the right answer but to the wrong question. The men stopped smiling, said something to each other, and they all nodded again with funny looks on their faces.

The first man, the one who had waved at the beginning, said something else to Utuyu, something that of course Utuyu didn't understand either. Whatever it was, it was something serious, because the man wasn't smiling. When he said whatever it was he said, he slowly shook his head. He didn't look angry, and he didn't wave Utuyu away like the man in the shop had done, but he looked like he didn't want to talk to Utuyu anymore. He turned his back and went on talking to his friends as though he didn't know Utuyu was there.

There were two women sitting at one of the tables. They had faces pale as the face of the woman in the glass box in Father Juan's church. They were eating eggs and beans and drinking coffee. They had a basket of flat bread in front of them, too. Utuyu went to their table. They looked at him in a friendly way, but they shook their heads and went on eating. Utuyu knew by now that people often did that until he started singing, so he stood right there, with his hands on the edge of their table, and began to sing.

The women stopped eating and looked at him. Then they looked at each other like they were surprised, and then they looked at him again. They looked pleased to begin with, but little by little the looks on their faces didn't look so pleased anymore. By the time Utuyu had finished his song, the women's faces looked like they had sucked on a sour lemon.

Utuyu started to sing another song, but one of the women put up her hand to make him stop. He went on singing anyway.

The woman quickly reached into her pocket and gave him a couple of coins. Utuyu went on singing.

She nodded her head up and down, up and down, like it was loose on her neck. Utuyu went on singing.

She smiled a smile at Utuyu that wasn't really a smile at all. He went on singing.

Finally the woman put up both her hands and waved them back and forth. Utuyu stopped singing, because he had come to the end of his song. The women went back to eating.

Utuyu was getting used to people pretending he wasn't there. It seemed to him a strange thing for people to want to pretend, because he was there all right. His stomach was starting to shout at him with a loud voice, and he was beginning to feel that kind of awful that hurt. He tapped one of the women on the arm. She looked up from eating, and her face looked like she'd eaten something she didn't like.

Utuyu pointed at the basket of flat bread.

In one quick, impatient move, the woman took all the flat bread out of the basket with two of her fingers and held it out to Utuyu at the very end of her arm. One of the men in white shirts and black pants was hurrying toward the table, and he was looking angry. Utuyu grabbed the bread and ran.

He sat on a bench on the far side of the square, eating the flat bread as fast as he could until his stomach had stopped shouting. This was turning out to be a different kind of day, a day when things weren't going the way they usually did. All the same, there was something familiar about this different day. Utuyu remembered everything had been quiet like this in the city before. There had been days when there hadn't been many people walking around, and when it had been easier to cross the streets because there weren't many cars and trucks and busses going by.

Utuyu thought about that. It had been a quiet day like this when he found the woman selling bread on the street, the woman who had let him sing and who had given him food. *This must be Sunday again,* Utuyu thought.

The woman had said she was always in the same place selling her bread on Sunday. So, if this was Sunday, the woman would be there again. Here in the square, nothing was happening, and people weren't being friendly at all. Utuyu decided he'd go find the woman who sold bread.

Chapter Fourteen

Utuyu had walked so many streets by now that he wasn't sure he could find the woman again. The place where she had been selling her bread had been close to a church, but everywhere you went in Oaxaca, there seemed to be a church nearby. Still, looking for churches was easier than looking for nothing at all. Utuyu was fairly sure the particular church he needed to find was in a certain direction from the biggest church of all—the one right there in the square. That's the direction he went. And sure enough, after Utuyu had looked up and down a few streets, that's where the woman was.

The woman looked glad to see Utuyu again, and Utuyu was glad to be with someone he could understand and who could understand him.

"Come sing!" the woman said. "No one's buying anything today. Maybe you can help."

But when Utuyu went up to her, her face changed just the way the other people's had.

"You know what?" she said, wrinkling her nose.

"What?" said Utuyu.

"You stink!" said the woman. "You're filthy, grubby dirty, and you stink! Worse than a pig sty full of rotten tomatoes! Don't you get anywhere near my bread! Stand over there and sing, over there where the people won't smell you and throw up."

So Utuyu went a little ways away and got ready to sing, but before he could start, the woman shouted at him. "Not over there! The air is blowing your stink all over me and my bread! Go over *there* where the air will blow your stink the other way."

Utuyu didn't feel very good about singing, but he sang anyway. At least he understood now why people had been so unfriendly so far that day. But stink or no stink, people stopped to listen to him singing. They always stood on one side of him, though, and not on the other. Some of them gave him coins, and some of them bought the woman's bread. At the end of the afternoon, the woman had sold a lot of her bread, and she bought Utuyu food to eat, just the way she said she would.

"We're going to have to do something about you," said the woman. "How long has it been since you washed yourself?"

Utuyu shrugged his shoulders. He really couldn't remember. The funny thing was that it was only other people who thought he stank. Utuyu had gotten so used to his own stink that he didn't notice it himself. Stinks can be that way.

As the woman was putting the rest of her bread in the basket she carried on her head, she said, "Come along with me. We've got to get you cleaned up." Utuyu started to go with her, but she said, "Stay behind me. A long way behind. And the air had better be blowing the right way."

Utuyu followed the woman into a part of the city he'd never seen before. After a while she stopped at a door and shouted. A little girl about Utuyu's age opened the door and the woman went in. Utuyu went in, too. There were two rooms inside, and children everywhere who ran up to the woman and hugged her legs.

"Stay away from him!" the woman said to the children. "This boy smells worse than a dog that's rolled in rotten cheese." All the children backed up and stared at Utuyu. Then they covered their noses and started laughing. Utuyu felt very unhappy. He stood in the middle of the room wishing he were somewhere else, somewhere like his room in the place behind the boards where no one could see him.

The woman got out a tub, put some water in it, and told Utuyu to get out of his filthy clothes. She put his shirt and pants into a plastic bag and closed it tight.

"Get in the tub," she ordered. Her voice was even more severe than Ita's when Ita was telling her children what to do. Utuyu did exactly what the woman said. He sat there in the tub while all the children stared at him, and the woman scrubbed him with soap and a rough cloth. She scrubbed him from top to bottom, from side to side and from front to back. She took the tub of dirty water to the door and threw it into the street, and then she put more water in the tub and scrubbed Utuyu's head so hard that he thought all his hair would come out. She scrubbed his head so hard that his eyes watered and he wanted to shout, but he squeezed his eyes tight and didn't make a sound.

"Well," finally said the woman, "that's better." She handed Utuyu a towel and told him to dry himself. Then she gave him another shirt and pair of pants.

The children started asking Utuyu all sorts of questions. They asked him how old he was, where he came from, how long he'd been in Oaxaca, where he was living, and how come he was in their house. Utuyu couldn't think of a single answer.

"He's in our house because he can sing, and when he sings, people buy more of my bread," said the woman. "He's here because he was stinking so badly that something had to be done about him."

"Is he going to live here?" asked a boy.

"He certainly is not," said the woman. "You think we have room for somebody else? And where's the food for that somebody else supposed to come from? Tell me that!"

Then she turned to Utuyu. "Off you go now, wherever it is you go. But here's what you're to do. You're to come here next Sunday morning, first thing, and give yourself another bath. Bring me my clothes back, and I'll give you yours back—that is, if they haven't all fallen apart by the time I've finished washing them. You understand?"

Utuyu nodded.

"You'd better understand," the woman said. "Otherwise I won't let you sing for me again."

Utuyu had sort of hoped the woman would let him sleep in her house that night, because he wasn't sure where he was, and now it was dark outside. He could see that wasn't going to happen, though.

The woman took him to the door. "You know how to get back to the square?"

"No," said Utuyu.

The woman told him how, and she also told him to remember how to get back to her house. At the door, she leaned down and gave him a kiss on one of his cheeks.

"Know what?" she said with a smile.

"What?" said Utuyu.

"You smell like a boy now," she said.

Utuyu found his way back to the square and was careful to notice the buildings he passed so he could find his way back to the woman's house again. From the square, he had no trouble getting to the place behind the boards. When he squeezed through the hole between the boards, though, he hadn't any idea how to find the flat space where his room was. It wouldn't have helped to climb to a high place on one of the rock hills, because it would have been too dark for him to see the green house in the distance. He'd have to wait until morning to find the flat space, and so he looked for a soft piece of ground just inside the boards, lay down, curled up, and went to sleep.

Chapter Fifteen

It seems to me that the way Utuyu chose to wait in the darkness showed that he was getting a lot smarter than he'd been at the beginning. It can be hard to wait when there's something we want to do right now, or somewhere we want to go right now, but for some reason we can't. Hard as it is, waiting a while can give time for the things that are stopping us to change.

For instance, by waiting through the night and letting the day begin again, Utuyu had no trouble finding his way back to his room in the flat space in the place behind the boards. Everything was just the way he'd left it. His money was safe in its plastic bag under the rock that was whiter than the rest, and his paper supply was still tucked into the broken part of the wall of his room.

That day, Utuyu felt lazy. One good thing about being there, in his own room with nobody around, was that because there wasn't anybody around, there wasn't anybody around to tell him he couldn't be lazy. He could be as lazy as he wanted to be. From the sounds in the distance, he could tell that the quiet day in the city was over. He could hear the cars and trucks and busses in the streets again, and he could imagine all the people walking here and there being busy about something. Right then, Utuyu didn't have to be busy about anything, so he sat in the early-morning sun in front of his room and was lazy.

You can sit in the sun and be lazy, but all the same your mind goes on thinking about something. Utuyu was thinking about how his life had taken a new shape there in the city of Oaxaca. He was thinking about how he had found ways to eat and drink and to get money. He still wasn't sure about how money worked once you'd found a way to get some, and he was thinking about that, too.

He was thinking about other things as well. He thought about how he had learned his way around the city, how to cross streets without getting squashed, and how to remember the way back to a place you wanted to go again. He was thinking about how he had learned to take care of his stomach when it shouted and his backside when it growled, and how he had found a way to wash and get clean so that people wouldn't make ugly faces.

Utuyu felt happy thinking about those things, and what made him happiest of all was thinking about how he had found a place to live, a safe place of his own, a place where he could sit in the sun and be lazy.

Those were all good things to think about, but there was something else that bothered him. How come he couldn't talk to most of the people in the city? How come they didn't understand him when he asked them something? How come he couldn't understand what they were saying? Thinking about that made Utuyu think of Gabriel. How come Gabriel could talk to the people, and the people could talk to him as well? Where was Gabriel, anyway? Where were Ita's children, for that matter? He never saw any of them around, not even Nino.

Utuyu still had some big questions to answer, but, if you ask me, I think he'd done a good job of finding out how to live in the city.

The days went by, one much the same as the other, except that each day seemed to get a little bit hotter than the one before. On the days when it was busy in the city, Utuyu spent his time finding what he needed to eat and drink. When the days became cooler and darker, he went to the square with the balloons and sang to the people at the tables. There were people who seemed to know him now when he came to the square—not only the men and women wearing black and white, but also some of the people at the tables. They would wave at him and motion with their hands for him to come and sing. When he'd finished singing to them, they gave him coins and food.

Once, some people with the pale, white faces motioned to him to sit with them at their table. They gave him part of what they were eating, and said something to one of the men in white shirts and black pants, and the man brought him a tall glass of fruit water. That was when Utuyu noticed that all the people at the tables were eating with knives and forks and spoons. He had no idea what those things were, or what they were called, or why the people didn't scoop up their food with the flat bread the way he did.

When he got back to his room, which he had no trouble finding now at night, he put the new coins in the plastic bag under the stone that was whiter than the rest.

Each time the quiet day came, Utuyu went first thing in the morning to the house of the woman who sold bread. He washed, and the woman gave him different clothes to wear. Then the two of them would go to the street corner next to the church. There, Utuyu would start singing again, and the woman would sell her bread. When there was no one to sing for, and no one was buying bread, the woman taught Utuyu new songs. He had a lot of songs to sing to people now.

No matter what you do, days don't stay the same for very long. You can try to stay the same and try to go on doing the same things every day, but new things are happening around you all the time, even when you're sleeping. Each day when you wake up, you can be sure that something new has happened. You may not see it right away, or for a while, but sooner or later, you'll bump into it. When you do, new things can happen in your life as well. At times, you can choose to let those new things change your life, or you can choose not to let them change it. It can be up to you to decide. At other times, there's nothing you can do about what changes. Either way, whether you choose to do something new, or something new just happens, you can never guess where that new thing will take you next.

One day, in the square with the balloons, Utuyu bumped into Gabriel again.

"Sky Boy!" said Gabriel, who looked surprised to see Utuyu. "You're still alive?"

"Where have you been?" Utuyu asked him. "I haven't seen you anywhere."

"I went back up in the mountains," Gabriel said. "It was time to help in the fields. And you? What have you been doing?"

"Finding my way around," Utuyu said.

Gabriel began asking him all sorts of questions, but Utuyu didn't always feel like he wanted to answer them. He didn't know why he didn't feel like answering them, but he knew for sure he didn't feel like it. He felt that maybe, if he answered too many of Gabriel's questions, he might lose something, although he didn't know what that something was.

"You got yourself any money?" asked Gabriel.

"Some," said Utuyu. "People give me money when I sing."

He certainly didn't feel like telling Gabriel about his plastic bag under the white stone.

"Where are you sleeping these days?" asked Gabriel. "Still sleeping in doorways?"

Utuyu certainly didn't feel like telling Gabriel about his room behind the boards, either.

"I found a park with bushes where no one can see me," said Utuyu. "I sleep there."

"So you're doing okay, are you?" said Gabriel. "That's good, Sky Boy. I guess you're an okay kid after all."

This was Utuyu's chance to find out about that thing that was bothering him, so he asked Gabriel how come he could talk to the people in Oaxaca when he, Utuyu, couldn't.

"Father Juan taught me how to do it," said Gabriel. "It took a while, but I learned how. They speak a different language here than we do in the mountains. You've got to learn their language if you want to be able to speak to them."

"Can I learn to do it?" Utuyu asked.

"You can learn to do whatever you want," said Gabriel, "so long as you've got someone to teach you. Like crossing the streets, remember? You learned how to do that, because you had someone to teach you. Me."

"Can Father Juan teach me to talk to the people?" Utuyu asked.

"He could if he had the time, but he's a busy guy," said Gabriel. "He's got a lot of stuff to do. You'd better find someone else to teach you."

"Can you teach me how?" asked Utuyu.

"No way," said Gabriel. "I'm a busy guy, too. I'm so busy I've gotta get going right now."

"What makes you so busy?" Utuyu asked.

"Making money, of course, dummy," said Gabriel. "That's what keeps everyone busy around here."

"How do you get the money?" asked Utuyu. "Do you have things to show the people, or what?"

"That's what I did when I was a squirt like you, but I don't have to do that anymore," said Gabriel. "Now I've got a bunch of kids just like you who do it for me. All I've got to do is run around and make sure they're working and not just sitting around doing nothing."

"Who gets to keep the money the people give them?" asked Utuyu.

"I do," said Gabriel. "I give some of it back to the kids, but I'm the guy who makes sure they've got enough to eat, somewhere to sleep at night, and stuff to sell. That takes money, too. Hey, Sky Boy, you want to be one of my kids?"

Utuyu thought about that for a moment, but it was only for a short moment. It was a short moment, but it was long enough for Utuyu to remember sitting in the sun, being lazy, and thinking good thoughts about all the things he'd learned to do. That short moment was also long enough for him to think about all his coins in the plastic bag under the white rock.

"Uh-uh," said Utuyu, "I guess not. Not right now. I'm doing okay, thanks."

"Suit yourself," said Gabriel, "but don't say I didn't give you the chance." Then Gabriel said, "See you 'round, Sky Boy!" and off he went.

Bumping into Gabriel like that was something new, something Utuyu didn't expect to happen. He didn't expect Gabriel to ask him to be one of his kids, either. If he had said "yes," if he had agreed to be one of Gabriel's kids, that would have changed Utuyu's life a lot. He would have had a new place to live, he would have had things to show the people, and Gabriel would have given him food every day. But he would have had to do what Gabriel told him, and he would have had to give Gabriel most of the money the people gave him.

This time, Utuyu had a choice. He could choose whether or not bumping into Gabriel like that would change his life. This time, Utuyu chose not to let it change anything.

Chapter Sixteen

Something else new happened to Utuyu one night in the square with the balloons. It was only a little thing, but it can be the little things you hardly notice at all when they happen that end up changing your life one day.

What happened was this. Utuyu was sitting by himself on one of the benches near the center of the square. He had been singing to the people at the tables, and one of them had given him some food to eat. He was sitting on the bench eating it, and he was wondering about the building that stood in front of him, right in the middle of the square. It wasn't like any of the other buildings around the square. To begin with, it didn't have any walls. It was open on all sides, with thin sticks that held up a huge roof with lights on the inside. The roof looked sort of like the hats the men who made the music wore. It was high in the middle, and then it spread out a long way on all sides.

There were stairs all around the building that you had to climb to get up under the roof. There were other stairs around the building, too, stairs that you could go down to get under the building. People were going up and down all these stairs all the time. Utuyu could understand why the people were going up the stairs to get under the roof, but he didn't understand why the people were going down the stairs to get underneath the whole building. What was going on down there?

That was what Utuyu was wondering when a man holding one of the great bunches of balloons walked over to him. Utuyu thought the man was going to ask him for some money for a balloon, but what the man said was:

"Hey, kid, hold these balloons for a minute, will you? I need to go to the bathroom."

The man said it in the language Utuyu could understand, which was lucky. If the man had said it in the other language Utuyu didn't understand, he would have had to guess what the man was saying. He'd have guessed the man wanted him to buy a balloon, and he'd have shaken his head to say "no." If he'd said "no," his life wouldn't have changed the way it was about to.

Instead, Utuyu said, "Sure."

The man handed Utuyu the bunch of balloons and hurried down one of the stairways that went underneath the building.

Now, Utuyu was closer to the balloons than he had ever been before. He had balloons over his head and all around him. He almost felt like he was inside a house made of balloons. The bunch of balloons was so big, and Utuyu was so small, that somebody walking by might have thought the bunch of balloons was tied to the bench and wouldn't have known that Utuyu was there at all.

The balloons had a special smell of their own. Utuyu knew that smell from the time Ita's children had brought balloons back from the city to Ita's house. The balloon the woman had given him when he first got to Oaxaca smelled like that, too. The smell wasn't like any other smell Utuyu knew. He'd have known that smell anywhere. If he'd smelled that smell in the middle of nowhere, he'd have known there were balloons around somewhere. With so many balloons surrounding him, the smell was strong. Utuyu liked it.

He liked having all the different shapes and colors of the balloons around him, too. Wherever he looked, there seemed to be a balloon he hadn't seen before. Until now, he hadn't ever seen the balloon that looked like an angry, green man, or the one that looked like a red man running, a man with a picture of a spider on his chest. If he turned his head a little, there was a smiling pig balloon, and turning his head the other way, a balloon in the shape of the moon when there's only a part of it in the sky at night.

Another thing Utuyu liked about holding the balloons was the way they pulled, gently, on his arm. They seemed almost alive in the way they moved and pulled. It was like they wanted to go somewhere, but Utuyu held on to them and told them they couldn't.

"Thanks, kid," the man said. He took back the bunch of balloons, and suddenly Utuyu was out of his balloon house and back in the square again.

"What goes on down there under the building?" Utuyu asked the man.

"You never been down there?" said the man. "How long have you been around?"

Utuyu didn't know whether to say "Not for long," or to say "For a long time." Being in Oaxaca seemed both ways to him.

"For a while," Utuyu said.

"They've got some stuff to eat and drink down there," said the man. "And they've got bathrooms you can use. It costs money, though. One of these." The man held up the coin with the wiggly edges. Utuyu had lots of those in his plastic bag. "But they give you paper if you need it," the man said.

The man seemed to like having someone to talk to. He talked and talked. He talked about how hot it was getting, and how some days there was water in the faucets where he lived, and some days there wasn't. He talked about his aches and pains, and how stiff he felt when he got up in the mornings. He talked about how different the city was now from the way it had been when he was a boy.

Utuyu didn't say a word. Even if he'd understood everything the man was saying, which he didn't, and even if he'd had something he wanted to say, it would have been hard to get the man to stop talking long enough to say anything at all. Utuyu started yawning, and he knew it was time to go back to his place behind the boards.

"Getting sleepy, huh?" said the man. "When you've got to sleep, you've got to sleep, right? Now me, I don't sleep much," he said, and then he began talking again, talking about the thoughts that went through his head when he wasn't sleeping, and the dreams he dreamt when he was.

Utuyu could hardly keep his eyes open anymore.

"Go to bed before you fall off the bench," the man finally said. "Where's your bed, anyway?" he asked.

Utuyu was still just awake enough to stop himself telling the man about the place behind the boards. He was still sleepy enough, too, so that he didn't feel like talking, anyway.

"It's over there a ways," he said. "It's not far."

"You're a good kid," said the man. "I enjoyed our talk. Here," he said, untying a purple balloon with a smiley face on it and giving it to Utuyu. "Keep smiling, rain or shine."

Utuyu fell right asleep as soon as he got to his room behind the boards. He liked knowing that his balloon would still be there this time when he awoke.

From then on, he often saw the same balloon man in the square, and more and more often, the man asked Utuyu to hold his balloons for a while. Sometimes the man would be gone only for a few minutes, but other times he'd be gone for a lot longer. When he was gone for a while, Utuyu would see him standing around with other men, talking.

Meeting the balloon man was another new thing Utuyu hadn't expected. It seemed like a small thing at the time. There was no way Utuyu could have known, or to have guessed, that it would turn out to be a big thing in the end.

Chapter Seventeen

The weather in Oaxaca is different from the weather that you're probably used to. It's certainly different from the weather where I live. Where I live, it gets warmer in the spring after a cold winter, and the trees grow new leaves again after not having had any leaves at all for a long time.

As spring becomes summer, it gets hot, and people begin thinking about going to the beach to swim and cool off. Then, as summer turns into autumn in September, the weather begins getting cooler again. People start wearing more clothes to keep warm, and little by little the leaves of the trees turn yellow and begin dropping off the branches until the branches are all bare. Then along comes winter, and it can get really cold. Out of the cupboards come the big sweaters and mittens. Out come the heavy snow boots. People light fires in the fireplace and stay indoors a lot.

Where I live, it can rain any old time. You never know when you're going to have a rainy day, and there can be several rainy days in a row. In the winter, that's true for snowy days as well.

The weather isn't like that in Oaxaca. In Oaxaca, it's always warm enough during the day to walk around without a sweater. There are always lots of trees that have leaves and flowers on them. No one keeps snow boots in the cupboard, because it's never, ever, snowed in Oaxaca. What the weather does in Oaxaca is go from warm to hot, and then from hot to hotter, and then back to warm again.

It doesn't rain much in Oaxaca, either. There's only one time of the year when people expect it to rain, and that's when we're having summer where I live. In Oaxaca, the rain begins when the weather has finished being as hot as can be and is getting ready to go back to being warm. That's when thick, dark clouds gather above the mountains in the late afternoon and come rolling down into the city. When they come, they can bring so much rain all at once that you can get soaking wet running from one side of the street to the other. But the rain only rains for a little while, and then it suddenly stops.

In Utuyu's room in the flat place behind the boards, it got so hot before the rains came that some days he didn't want to leave the room at all. He would go out only in the evening when the fierce sun had left the sky. He would be sure to find enough food during the evening to last him through the next hot day, so that he could stay in the shade of his room.

One evening, at the end of a very hot day, Utuyu was singing, as usual, to the people in the square with the balloons. The sky grew dark much earlier than normal. With a clap of thunder, down came buckets of rain. Almost everyone walking around in the square ran for cover. Some ran up the steps to get under the roof that looked like a hat on the building in the middle, and some ran down the steps that went under the building. Men jumped out of the tall chairs where they were having their shoes shined and ran for cover. The men who were shining the shoes covered their chairs with plastic bags and ran for cover, too. The balloon sellers found empty spaces in the arches around the square where they and their bunches of balloons could fit and stay dry.

People crowded around the tables where people sat and watched the rain come down. The only people left in the square were people who had big umbrellas and were hurrying to get somewhere, and here and there a few children danced and jumped about in the rain, shouting and laughing. Everyone looked pleased. Everybody was smiling and talking to each other as though something wonderful had happened.

The rain didn't last long. It went away as fast as it had come, as if the buckets in the sky were suddenly empty. Everything in the square returned to the way it had been before. All the people who had acted like something wonderful was happening when the rain began, acted as if nothing had happened at all. The only thing that was different now was that everything was wet and shiny.

Utuyu looked around to see where he could start singing again. A man sitting alone at one of the tables motioned for Utuyu to come over to where he was sitting. The man had a black beard, and Utuyu thought he had seen the man before somewhere, but he couldn't remember where. When Utuyu got to the man's table, the man surprised him by talking to him in the language he understood. He surprised Utuyu more by saying:

"You're the Sky Boy, aren't you? You're Utuyu."

Utuyu nodded and wondered how the man could know his name.

"Your friend, Gabriel, has told me about you," said the man.

Then Utuyu remembered where he had seen the man. He'd seen the man standing in the big room in the church, wearing fancy clothes and talking to the people. Utuyu stood there, looking at Father Juan. He couldn't think of anything to say, because he wasn't sure how he felt. When this man spoke, he could make people stand up and kneel down when he wanted to. They did what he told them to do, and Utuyu wondered if Father Juan was going to tell him to do something now.

Father Juan did.

"Sit with me for a minute," Father Juan said, and Utuyu, without thinking about it, sat down at the table.

"Are you hungry? Thirsty?" Father Juan asked.

Utuyu nodded. Father Juan said something to one of the men in white shirts and black pants, something in the language Utuyu didn't understand. Utuyu thought maybe Father Juan had told the man to kneel down, but the man didn't. Instead, the man nodded his head and went away.

"You're a good singer, Utuyu," Father Juan said. "Everyone's getting to know you around here. How did you learn?"

"I sang when I was at Ita's house," said Utuyu. "And the woman who sells bread teaches me new songs."

"I see," said Father Juan. "So you just knew how. That's a lucky gift, isn't it? Not everyone can do that." Then Father Juan asked, "Who do you live with? Who looks after you?"

Utuyu had that feeling again that he should be careful about what he said or he might lose something.

"No one," said Utuyu, but he didn't feel like saying anything more.

"So you look after yourself, do you?" said Father Juan. "That's hard work. It's especially hard work when you can't talk to most of the people, no?" said Father Juan.

Father Juan was certainly right about that, and before he could stop himself, Utuyu said:

"Gabriel says you taught him how to do it, but you won't teach me how because you're too busy."

The man in the white shirt and black pants came back to the table with a plate of beans, rice and chicken, and a glass of fruit water, too. He put the plate and the glass in front of Utuyu, along with a knife and fork. Utuyu looked at Father Juan, not sure what he should do.

"Eat," said Father Juan.

Utuyu looked at the knife and fork.

"You don't need those," said Father Juan, and he gave Utuyu a piece of flat bread.

"Eat," he said again.

So Utuyu started eating the only way he knew how, with the flat bread and his fingers. He ate as fast as he could in case the man decided to come back and take the plate away again.

"Gabriel's right," said Father Juan. "I can't teach you how to talk to the people, but I can tell you where you can go, where other people can teach you. That is, if you really want to learn."

Utuyu thought about that and went on eating.

"You don't have to if you don't want to," said Father Juan. "Learning how is hard work, too, and you seem to be getting along fine."

Utuyu felt he'd better say something, and quickly, or Father Juan wasn't going to tell him where that place was.

"I want to learn how," said Utuyu.

"Okay, then," said Father Juan, and while Utuyu was scooping up the last of the rice and beans on his plate, Father Juan wrote something on a piece of paper. When he'd finished writing, he folded up the paper and gave it to Utuyu. "This says what the place is called and where it is. It also tells the people there that I know you, and that I'd like them to take you in and help you start learning."

Utuyu took the paper, but because he couldn't read, he wondered how he was supposed to find the place. Father Juan seemed to know what he was thinking.

"See that building over there at the corner of the square? The big, pink one?"

Utuyu nodded.

"You walk down the street next to the building, and when you get to the fifth street going across, you turn right." Father Juan took Utuyu's right hand and squeezed it. "That way," he said. "Will you remember?"

Utuyu nodded. That was the hand he used most, and that was what he'd remember.

"You turn that way, and when you get to the second street going across, you show the paper to someone. They'll tell you where to go after that."

Utuyu was putting the paper in his pocket, when another man came up to the table, a man Father Juan was glad to see, because he jumped up and gave the man a big smile and a hug.

"Off you go now, Utuyu," said Father Juan. "This man and I have things we have to talk about now."

Utuyu nodded, but he didn't really want to go.

"You know the church where I work, right?"

Utuyu nodded again.

"Come find me if you need to."

That made Utuyu feel better, so he started to leave. "The food was good. Thanks," he said.

"You're welcome," said Father Juan. "You can come and sing for me sometime in return, right?"

"Sure," said Utuyu, and then he set off for his room behind the boards.

Chapter Eighteen

There are times when everything's going along just fine, when you're thinking you know what's going to happen each day and how tomorrow will turn out. You know when you'll get up in the morning, when you'll eat and play, and when the people you love will go away for a while and then come back again. At the end of the day, you know when it's time to get back in bed again and go to sleep, before the next day begins the same way as the one you left behind when you closed your eyes. And then, WHAMO!, along comes something that turns everything upside down. All at once you have to learn new and different ways of doing the same old things.

Lots of children find they suddenly have to move to a new place to live. A Mom or a Dad might get a new job to do in a town far away, and then, just when you thought you knew how school worked, and who your best friends were, you have to pack up, go away, and start finding out how things work all over again.

These sorts of changes can be hard for a while, but lots of the time they bring good new adventures—as Utuyu was about to find out. Getting used to new things means we're growing, and Utuyu still had a lot of growing to do.

Not long after the evening when Utuyu had talked with Father Juan in the square with the balloons, one of his days began differently from the others. There was a noise of loud engines nearby and then a lot of banging. In his house in the flat space behind the boards, no day had begun like that before, so Utuyu went out to see what was happening. From the top of one of the piles of stone, he could see tractors and bulldozers right where he always squeezed through the boards. Men with large hammers were starting to knock those boards down. Utuyu didn't like the look of what he saw, and neither did the brown dog with the white face on the roof of the yellow building. He was barking angrily at the tractors and the bulldozers and the men, and this time he wasn't wagging his tail.

From then on, that's how Utuyu's mornings began—with lots of engine noise and lots of barking and banging. He found a new place to get in and out of the flat space so that the people wouldn't see him coming and going. Each day he went by the old place, he could see the tractors and bulldozers had pushed their way further and further inside. Each day they took away more and more of the piles of rocks, making a new flat space that was growing bigger and bigger right next to the street.

If they don't stop pushing their way in like this, Utuyu thought, *they're going to push their way right into my house! Then what am I supposed to do?*

At first, Utuyu didn't want to think about that, because he didn't have any idea what he was supposed to do if that happened. But the men and the machinery didn't stop, and the new flat space was getting bigger all the time, coming nearer to his house every day.

Now, it was easier for Utuyu to tell when it was Sunday and he was supposed go to the house of the woman who sold bread. On Sundays, the day began just like it used to begin. There were no noisy engines and no banging of hammers. Even the dog on the roof of the yellow house didn't bark on Sundays. But making Sunday easier to know was the only good thing Utuyu could find in what was happening. Between Sundays, the new flat space kept coming nearer to where he lived.

There came one day when the new flat space had come so close that Utuyu could hear the men shouting to each other when they were working. He knew he couldn't go on *not* thinking about what he was supposed to do next, because the time when he was going to have to find something to do next was coming in a hurry. So, sitting in the warmth of the sun one quiet Sunday, he decided to think about it. The only thought that came to his mind right then was to ask the woman who sold bread if he could go live in her house. She'd already said "no" once, but that had been a while ago, and maybe by now she'd have changed her mind.

So, after he'd taken his bath at her house, and the two of them were together out on the street by the church, and lots of people were buying bread, and Utuyu could see the woman was in a good mood, Utuyu asked the woman if, maybe, sometime soon, he could come live with her and her children.

The woman looked at him and said "no" again. She had too many children to look after, she said, and not enough food or money to look after another one.

When that plan didn't work, Utuyu had to think of another. He thought of asking Gabriel if he'd still let him be one of his gang. Utuyu thought about that for a while, but as he thought about it, he could feel that he didn't feel any better about the idea than he had before. Why should he have to give Gabriel the money he got by singing? He already knew how to get the food he needed, so he didn't need Gabriel to get it for him. It was just the problem of where to live, and Utuyu decided that if he had to, he could always go back to living under the bushes in the park. He didn't know how to find Gabriel, anyway, but if he bumped into him by accident one of these days, Utuyu decided he wouldn't ask if he could be one of Gabriel's gang—at least, not yet.

Then Utuyu thought about Father Juan. Gabriel had said Father Juan had a place for children to live. He'd said there was no room there, but that had been a while ago, too. Maybe things had changed since then. Maybe there would be room at Father Juan's place now. Because it was Sunday, Utuyu knew just where Father Juan would be—in the church where he worked on Sundays—and so that's where Utuyu went.

When Utuyu got to the church, Father Juan was there all right, but he was standing at the far end of the big room where he had been before, standing in front of the woman who was all dressed up in the glass box. Father Juan was talking to the people in front of him in the loud, strange voice Utuyu remembered from before. He was still telling them when to sit and kneel and stand, and when to sing. After a while, everyone sat back in their seats, and Father Juan walked up some steps to a platform higher than the people's heads. That's when he saw Utuyu standing in the doorway. His loud, strange voice that seemed to come from everywhere said, in Utuyu's own language, "Come in, Utuyu. Come in and sit down." The people all looked at each other, and then they looked over their shoulders to where Father Juan was pointing, and that meant they were all looking right at Utuyu. Utuyu felt very small, standing there alone in the big door with everyone looking at him.

"Have you come to see me?" Father Juan's loud voice said.

Utuyu nodded.

"Then come in and sit down and wait for me," said Father Juan's loud voice.

Everyone was still staring at him, so to stop them staring, Utuyu went into the big room and sat down. Everyone turned around again to look at Father Juan, and Father Juan talked to them for what seemed to Utuyu like a long time. When he'd finished talking, Father Juan walked down the steps and began telling the people what to do again. Utuyu did whatever the people did whenever they did it, because he didn't want them staring at him anymore. He stayed sitting when they stayed sitting, and he kneeled on his knees when they did, and he stood up when they did, and he tried to sing when they started singing. He wasn't able to sing very well, though, because he didn't know any of the songs.

Utuyu stayed in the big room doing whatever the people did for what seemed like forever. He looked around at the sad pictures on the walls. He looked at the woman in the glass box and wondered what she was doing there. There was a strange, sweet smell in the air, and he wondered where it was coming from. He looked at Father Juan and wondered why he was dressed up in strange clothes. Utuyu's head started itching, but he didn't know if he should scratch it or not. His legs, which didn't touch the floor when he was sitting, started feeling cold and prickly, so he swung them back and forth. One of his feet hit the back of the seat in front of him with a loud BANG! that went right around the room. The person in the seat turned and glared at him. Utuyu was glad whenever Father Juan told everyone they had to stand up.

And then, at last, whatever was going on seemed to be coming to an end, because Father Juan stopped talking, and everyone started gathering up their things around them. But then Father Juan's loud voice said something else, and everyone stopped getting ready to leave and turned to stare at Utuyu again.

"Utuyu," said Father Juan's loud voice, "you owe me a song, remember?"

Utuyu nodded.

"How about you sing it for me now? For all of us."

Utuyu slowly shook his head. That didn't seem to him like a good idea.

"Come now, Utuyu," said Father Juan's loud voice. "You don't have to sing for us if you really don't want to, but we would all like it very much if you would. And then you and I can talk for as long as you want."

That changed Utuyu's mind about singing, and what's more, the people started calling out to him and clapping their hands. So Utuyu stood up and began to sing, but he'd only just begun when Father Juan's loud voice stopped him. "Wait, Utuyu," said Father Juan. "You'll have to come up here or no one will be able to hear your song."

Utuyu didn't feel like going up there where Father Juan was standing, but he did, hurrying between the rows of people and looking at his feet so that he wouldn't have to look at the people's faces. When he reached Father Juan, he felt a little bit better, especially when Father Juan put an arm around him and said, in a quiet voice no one else could hear, "Thank you, Utuyu. I'm right here with you, and it's all right."

Then Father Juan gave him the microphone that made his voice sound so loud and told him to hold it close to his mouth when he sang. As soon as he sang the very first note of his song, Utuyu understood what a microphone did.

That first note filled the big room and seemed to come from everywhere, even from the ceiling high over his head. As he went on singing, Utuyu wondered if it really was his voice that he was hearing. It seemed to him it had to be, because whenever he ran out of breath and had to take another gulp of air, the voice all around him in the big room did the same thing, too.

Everyone was still and quiet. Utuyu's song was only a short song, and when he came to the end of it, someone called out something, everyone nodded, and Father Juan asked him to sing it again. This time, when he came to the end of his song, everyone clapped and smiled.

Father Juan squatted down and gave Utuyu a hug. "You see how happy you have made us?" he said. "Our happiness makes Our Lady happy as well," he said, pointing to the woman in the glass box. Utuyu didn't think the woman in the glass box looked any happier or sadder than she had before, but he didn't say anything about it. All he knew was that he liked the way his voice went flying around the room, as though it were an invisible songbird on great wings. He liked it so much that he hoped Father Juan would ask him sometime to let that songbird fly through the big room again.

Chapter Nineteen

When everyone had left the church, Father Juan took Utuyu into a small room. There were a table and two chairs—not counting the one behind the table where Father Juan went to sit.

"Sit down," said Father Juan, pointing to one of the chairs. Utuyu sat. It seemed to him that Father Juan liked telling people to get up or sit down.

"What's up?" said Father Juan.

Utuyu didn't know how to begin. He looked around the room, wondering what to say. There were books on the walls, and there were more sad pictures, and there was a scary-looking thing made out of wood. It was a man whose hands and feet had been nailed to a board, and the man didn't look happy about it at all. In fact, he looked like maybe he was dead. Even if Utuyu had known what to say, this room would have made him too scared to say it. All he could do was stare at Father Juan.

Father Juan seemed to understand. "Would you feel better if we went and talked outside?" he asked.

Utuyu nodded, and he did feel a lot better when he and Father Juan were sitting on the edge of a fountain under a tree. In fact he felt so much better that he was able to tell Father Juan about the flat space behind the boards, and how he didn't think he'd have anywhere to live anymore.

"That's tough luck," said Father Juan. "And just when you seemed to be getting along fine. I'm sorry."

Utuyu waited for Father Juan to tell him he could come live at his place, wherever that was, but Father Juan didn't. For a while, neither of them said anything, and then Utuyu said, "Gabriel said you had somewhere for kids to live."

"That's true," said Father Juan, "but here's how it is: There are lots and lots of children in Oaxaca just like you, children with nowhere to live. I wish I could give them all somewhere to live, but I can't. I don't have room for them."

"I'm little," said Utuyu. "I don't take up much room."

"I know," said Father Juan. "But there are already more kids in that house than the house can hold. Some are much littler than you. And I've already made promises to many other kids that as soon as there's room in the house, they can come live there. I have to keep those promises."

So this isn't going to work, either, thought Utuyu.

Then Father Juan asked Utuyu if he'd gone to the place he'd told him about, the place where they could teach him to speak the language Utuyu didn't understand. Utuyu shook his head. As a matter of fact, he'd forgotten all about it.

"I'd go there, if I were you," said Father Juan. "You need to be able to speak that language, and maybe someone there will know of somewhere for you to live."

Then Utuyu said, "Can I come sing here again?"

"I'd like that," said Father Juan. He pulled on his beard for a moment, and then said, "I'll make a deal with you. If you'll go to that place I told you about, you can come and sing here the first Sunday of every month."

"When's that?" asked Utuyu. "I don't know when that is."

Father Juan smiled. "No, of course you don't. But you'll learn what it is if you'll go where I told you. I'll tell you what. Come sing here the first Sunday after you've seen the moon is full. How about that?"

Utuyu nodded.

"You've still got the paper I gave you?" asked Father Juan.

Utuyu didn't know if he did or he didn't. Maybe it was stuffed in the crack in the wall in his house in the flat space, and maybe it wasn't. He shrugged his shoulders.

Father Juan took Utuyu back to the scary room and wrote it all down again for him. "Don't lose it this time, Utuyu," he said. "And the people there are going to tell me if you show up or not, and that means if you can come sing here or not. We've got a deal, remember?"

Utuyu nodded and put the piece of paper in his pocket.

"Do you remember how I told you to get there?" asked Father Juan.

Utuyu didn't remember, but he was starting to feel dumb again, the way Gabriel had made him feel dumb, so he pretended he did remember and nodded his head to show he did.

"Before you go now," said Father Juan, "go up to Our Lady in the church and ask her to help you find somewhere to live. Just look at her in the eyes and ask. You don't have to ask out loud. She'll know what you're thinking. You'd be surprised what she can do." Then he said, "Good luck, Utuyu. Let me know what happens." He patted Utuyu on the head and went off back to his work.

Utuyu sat on the edge of the fountain for a moment or two, thinking. He walked over to the door of the church and looked in. The big room looked bigger than ever with no one in it. At the far end, there was the woman in the glass box.

If Father Juan can't help me, what's that woman in her box going to be able to do? Utuyu wondered. *She's not even a real person!*

He looked at the woman at the far end of the big room and decided he didn't want to go any closer.

"Go ahead, then," he said quietly to the woman in the box. "So go ahead, lady, and find me somewhere to live if you can!"

Utuyu turned around and went into the street. He walked back to his home in the flat space, feeling sad and angry at the same time. While he'd been gone, the men and machinery had pushed their way closer.

Utuyu went to the big square late that afternoon. He didn't feel like singing. He sat on a bench and watched the square growing dark around him. People were coming and going the way they always did, and they all looked happy.

Can you remember a time when you felt sad or mad about something, and everyone around you was talking and smiling and laughing as if there was nothing wrong?

If you can remember a time like that, you know how Utuyu was feeling right then. He felt mad at the people. He wished they'd all go away. He crossed his arms and frowned at the ground, pretending the people weren't there. He swung his legs back and forth, pretending he was kicking something—and kicking it hard. There he sat, kicking the air and staring at his old sandals as they kicked back and forth. There was something different about his sandals. They looked smaller on his feet than they used to. Or was it that his feet looked bigger in his sandals than they used to? He noticed something else different about his sandals and his feet. They almost touched the ground now. For a moment, Utuyu's frown went away.

"Hey, kid," shouted a voice. "Come over here a minute!" It was the man with the balloons, the one who liked to talk so much. Right then, Utuyu didn't feel like listening to the man—or to anyone at all, for that matter. He frowned at the man and shook his head. The man didn't seem to understand, because he came right over to where Utuyu was sitting.

"What's the matter with you today, kid?" he asked. "You look like you just swallowed a sour lemon."

Utuyu frowned harder at the man and didn't say anything.

"Or sat on a prickly pear," the man said.

Utuyu still didn't say anything.

"Or, or . . . . Or asked your grandmother to scratch your head and she kicked you in the butt instead."

Utuyu tried not to smile, but he couldn't help smiling a little. "I haven't got a grandmother," he said.

"So you're in a bad mood about something," said the man. "You know what I used to do when I was a kid and was in a bad mood? I'd go out in the field to a place where there were always scorpions, and I'd push two of them together with a stick until they started fighting with each other."

"I used to do that, too," said Utuyu.

"Kids are alike," said the man. "Of course, they're all different, too. What would a city kid know about scorpions except to stay out of their way 'cause they're mean and can sting you?"

"They're not mean," said Utuyu, remembering his times with the scorpions at the rock pile at Ita's house. "They're just scorpions, that's all."

"You're one smart kid," said the man.

"What we do is up to us, right?" said Utuyu. "We're supposed to get to decide."

"You'd better believe it!" said the man. "So I'd make the scorpions fight, and I'd stay there until one of them was dead. Then I'd feel a whole lot better. It was like my bad mood was the scorpion that got killed. So let's hear it. What scorpion's inside you today, kid?" said the man. "What's made you so mad?"

Utuyu didn't know whether to tell the man or not, so he just said, "I'm getting pushed out of my place, and I've got to find a new place to live. I don't even get to decide about it. That's what."

"Well, how about that!" said the man. "I'll tell you something, kid. Things always happen for a reason. They don't happen just because they happen, they happen so something else can happen that wouldn't have happened if they hadn't happened in the first place. Know what I mean?"

Utuyu didn't have any idea what the man meant.

"Like I remember a time when I woke up one day and my father was gone," the man went on. "He was gone a lot of the time, but this time he was, like *gone.* He didn't come back. Gone for good. That was a really bad thing that happened. Us kids were all left alone with our mother, and there was no one to bring us money for food or anything. You know what happened that wouldn't ever have happened if that hadn't happened? I'll tell you what. One day our mother packed us all up and took us here to the city. I wouldn't have ever seen the city if my father hadn't gone."

"What's so great about seeing the city?" said Utuyu. "I think it sucks."

"If you want to know something that really sucks," said the man, reaching into his pocket, "try this. Here." He gave Utuyu a lollipop wrapped in green paper. "As for Oaxaca, no way it sucks! Look at me," said the man. "Here I am today, and I've got a good life. I learned to fix cars, and that's something I'd never have learned if I hadn't come to the city. I've got a bunch of people who sell my balloons, and I get some extra money from that so

I can go out with my friends and have a drink. I've even got a wife who looks after me, know what I mean?"

"You got kids?" Utuyu asked the man.

"No kids," said the man.

"Why not?" said Utuyu. "Everyone has kids."

"Not everyone," said the man. "Some of us are lucky. Now I don't mean kids aren't fine and all that, no, I don't mean that at all, Hey look at you. You're a good kid. But kids take money, and they keep you at home, and you've got to look after them, right? Now me, I can do what I want. It's up to me. The way I look at it, I'm better off the way I am."

Utuyu thought about that for a while, and then he had an idea. "You got room for a kid where you live?" he asked the man. "Maybe just for a while?"

"Sorry kid," said the man. "No room. We've got a place just big enough for the two of us. My wife wants a dog, but we haven't even got room for a dog. Not even a little dog. Not even a dog as big as a cat. Not even for a cat that's as big as a mouse."

Didn't anyone have any room, Utuyu wondered? If that's the way it was in Oaxaca, he thought, maybe he'd better go back to Ita's house and see if there was any room for him there now. But suppose there wasn't? What would he do then?

"Like I said, kid," the man went on, "things happen for a reason. You know why I think you're getting pushed out of your place?"

"Why?" said Utuyu.

"So that you'll have a problem, and it's a problem that can solve a problem *I've* got. It's like this," said the man. "I've got to find someone to look after my balloons at night. I don't know what's going on, but some days there are balloons missing when I open the place in the morning and my people come to get them. I've got to find someone who's going to stay there at night and make some noise, you know, keep an eye on things."

"I could do that!" said Utuyu. "I could make noise and stuff."

"I think you could, I think you could," said the man, "and have I ever got a deal for you!"

This was turning out to be a funny kind of day, Utuyu thought. Everyone wanted to make a deal. First there was Father Juan's deal, and now this man had a deal to make.

"What kind of deal?" Utuyu asked.

"Here's the deal," said the man. "You stay with my balloons at night. You've got to be there when the people bring their balloons back at night, and you've got to be there when they come for them in the morning, and you've got to stay there with the balloons in between. Other than that, you can do what you want. You can go on singing, because all the balloons are out there in the square then. And you know what?"

"What?" said Utuyu.

"I'll pay you money if you take good care of my balloons. Not much money, but, hey, you get a roof over your head, and you get to earn money when you're asleep! How are you going to find a better deal than that?"

The man's deal sounded good to Utuyu. Any deal about a place to live would have sounded good to Utuyu right then, but this sounded like a *really* good deal. So the man and Utuyu agreed on how the deal would work, and they agreed that Utuyu would start his new job the very next night. The man told him to get what he had where he was living now and bring it to the square in the morning. The man would show him where he kept his balloons and where Utuyu was to stay. When they'd agreed on everything, Utuyu felt like singing again.

"See what I mean, kid," said the man. "Everything happens for a reason."

Utuyu woke up early in the flat space the next morning. He gathered his things together, and that only took a couple of minutes, because he didn't have much to gather up—just his supply of paper stuffed in the crack in the wall, and the plastic bottle he used for water, and the food he'd saved for the next day. He wrapped all that in a piece of old blanket he'd found one night in a trashcan, and when he had everything wrapped up in a bundle, he sat in the sun and thought about what was coming next.

He wondered about what his new place would be like. He knew his life would certainly be different now, but he couldn't imagine exactly how. All he could see in his imagination was a room full of balloons, and that was a happy thing to imagine. As for all the rest, who could tell? But at least he'd have a place to live again.

Part of him was sad to be leaving his home in the flat space. He'd gotten used to being there, and it had been his very own. He'd found it all by himself, and he'd found out all by himself how to live there and be happy. He'd miss the familiar sound of the barking dog on the roof of the yellow building, and he'd miss having his very own lazy days when he could stay here in the flat space, here in the sun, and do nothing at all. He'd miss the times when it rained. He'd miss watching the rain making waterfalls down the piles of rocks until the sun came back out again and made the rocks dry again in no time at all.

Rocks! He suddenly remembered the plastic bag with his money under the rock that was whiter than the rest. He went and got it, and when he'd tucked it safely into the blanket along with his other things, he took a last look around. He could hear the men and the machinery working away right nearby.

'Bye, flat space, he thought.

It was still early, and maybe the balloon man wouldn't be in the big square yet, but Utuyu decided he'd go there anyway and wait. With his blanket bundle on his shoulder, he walked straight out toward where the boards had been, the boards he'd squeezed through at the very beginning. When he passed the men and machinery, the men stopped their work and stared at him, wondering where he'd suddenly come from. When he got to the street, the dog was up there on the roof of the yellow building, looking down. When the dog saw Utuyu, he didn't bark. He just whined a little.

Utuyu looked up at the dog. "See you," he said. The dog wagged his tail. Then Utuyu walked off in the direction of the big square.

As it turned out, Utuyu left the flat space just in time. Two days later, the men and machinery cleared away the last pile of rocks and knocked Utuyu's old house down, right down to the ground.

Chapter Twenty

If it seems to you that Utuyu is acting differently now than he acted at the beginning of the story, I'd agree with you. When he left the flat space for the last time that morning, he was walking differently than he walked when he first got to Oaxaca. If you'd been a bird high up in the air when Utuyu first came to Oaxaca, you'd have seen a little boy—a *very* little boy—wandering around the streets of the city, looking like he didn't know where he was going, and acting like he was afraid of everything. But if you'd been that same bird looking down at Utuyu leaving the flat space with his blanket bundle, I think you'd have seen a boy who was a lot bigger. I think you might have said to yourself, "Now there's a boy who looks like he knows exactly where he's going and how to get there—a boy who doesn't look afraid of anything at all!"

That's because a lot of time had passed since Utuyu first came to the city. I haven't told you about all the days that went by in Utuyu's life in Oaxaca, because many of them were the same as the last one and the same as the next one, and nothing special happened to tell you about. Even when the days were the same, though, Utuyu was growing. When he was sleeping between the days, he was growing. He was growing taller, and he was growing stronger, and he was growing out of his shirts and pants and sandals. When he went to get a bath at the house of the woman who sold bread, the woman would shake her head and give him a shirt he'd never worn before. Her children were growing, too, and that was lucky, because there was always a shirt one of them had grown out of that Utuyu could wear.

The woman who sold bread hadn't grown taller, though. She'd stopped growing a long time ago. Children can do lots of things that grownups can't do anymore, and growing taller is one of them. When Utuyu first came to the city, he'd been about six. Now he was about eight. He was still the same boy. Growing doesn't change that. But his outside had changed, just the way your outside is changing as you're growing taller, too.

Utuyu's new home was one big room with a tin roof. It was way bigger than his old room had been. In fact, it was bigger than Ita's whole house. There was a flat space around it that was like the flat space around his old room, but the new flat space was much bigger than the old one as well.

During the day, people drove cars into the flat space and left them there. Later on in the day, they came and got their cars again. In the daytime, the man who sold balloons was there. He didn't have much time to talk, though. He'd say good morning to Utuyu when he came in the morning, and ask him if everything had been okay during the night, and then he'd sit in a wooden box next to the street for a while, eating a piece of bread and drinking from a plastic cup. He'd give the people pieces of paper when they brought in their cars, and when the people came back for their cars again, they'd give the man money. When no one was bringing cars, the man was busy fixing some of the cars the people had left. He'd open up the front of a car, stick his head in, and stay that way for a long time. Or he'd lie underneath one of the cars, so that Utuyu could see only the man's feet sticking out.

In one corner of the empty space there was a place behind a wall, without a roof but where no one could see you. That's where the man told Utuyu he could go to the bathroom when he had to. There was an old toilet there, but although it was old, it was altogether new to Utuyu. He'd never seen one before, but he figured out what it was for and how to use it.

There was an old mattress in his new room. Sleeping on it was much more comfortable than sleeping on the ground. It was so comfortable that Utuyu often didn't want to get up in the morning. He'd hear the church bells ringing, and he'd see the bright daylight coming through the door and through cracks between pieces of the tin roof, but he'd turn over on his other side and go right back to sleep again. Some days he was still asleep when the man came to open up the wooden box where he sat by the street.

Utuyu especially liked the nights there. He liked being there when the people brought their bunches of balloons back from the big square. In they'd come, one by one, some with their children, and their bunches of balloons would fill all the space up against the tin roof. By the time the last person had come and left the last bunch of balloons, Utuyu couldn't see the tin roof at all. He'd lie on his mattress and look up, and it was like the whole sky was made of balloons. It was dark, of course, but there were lights all night outside around the flat space.

In his room, lying on his back on his mattress, Utuyu could still see the shapes and colors of the balloons above him—the dog balloons and the cat balloons, the tiger balloons and the fish balloons, the airplane balloons and the balloons with faces on them. Here and there he could see the red balloons that looked like a man with a spider web on his front, and the green ones that looked like a man who was really mad at somebody about something.

Some children might have found the shapes of the balloons scary, particularly at night, but not Utuyu. He felt like the balloons were his friends and were keeping him company. He liked feeling that he was there to look after his friends, to take good care of them. He'd lie there on his mattress and make up stories about the balloons until he fell asleep, until his stories about the balloons turned into his dreams.

Everything was different in the daytime when the people took the balloons away to the big square. The room was empty. Well, it wasn't really empty, because there were pieces of old cars lying around in piles, and there were tires, and rubber tubes, and metal cables, and all kinds of tools hanging on the walls. Utuyu didn't mind leaving his supply of paper or food next to his mattress, but he didn't feel so happy leaving his bag with his money there. Soon after he moved in, he found an empty, tin box behind one of the piles of pieces of cars, and from then on, that's where he kept his money.

One day, Utuyu was wandering around the city, and he passed the church where Father Juan worked. That made him think of the lady in the glass box. Had she really helped him find a place to live, like Father Juan said she could? Utuyu didn't know, but as he passed the door of the church, he looked in. The lady was still there, looking just as she had before. Utuyu stood in the doorway, and he said, in a whisper, "If you did have anything to do with finding me a new home, thanks. I like it."

Passing Father Juan's church made Utuyu think about something else—about singing in the church again. That thought brought another thought along with it. Father Juan had said he wasn't going to let him sing unless he went to the place he'd written down on the piece of paper. A full moon had already come and gone by the time that thought came to Utuyu, but there would be another full moon before long. Utuyu decided he'd better find the place written on the paper and see what it was all about.

The next day, when all the balloons had gone and he was free to do whatever he wanted to do, Utuyu took Father Juan's piece of paper with him in his pocket. He couldn't remember how Father Juan had told him to get to the place, but it wasn't hard to find. Utuyu did remember which way Father Juan had told him to start from the big square, and so that's the way Utuyu began. When he didn't know which way to go next, he showed the paper to a policeman, and the policeman pointed, so that's the way Utuyu went next. He kept on showing the paper to people, and the people kept on pointing, until the last person he showed it to pointed to a door right across the street from where he was standing.

The door was shut, but Utuyu could hear the sounds of children running around and shouting inside. He knocked on the door and waited, but no one came to open it. He knocked on the door again and waited, but still no one came. *Maybe this isn't the right place after all,* he thought, *or if it is the right place, maybe they don't want anyone to come in.* He was about to go away, when the door opened to let a man out. A woman inside waved to the man as he left, and when she saw Utuyu, she said, "How long have you been standing out there, my small friend?"

"A while," Utuyu said. "The door was shut."

"Doors that are shut are doors made to knock on," said the woman.

"I did knock," said Utuyu.

"This is a door you have to knock on hard!" said the woman, and banged so hard on the door with the flat of her hand that she made Utuyu jump. "The thing is, we make a lot of noise in here some of the time, as you can see, and so you have to be noisier still if you want someone to hear you. Now come right in and tell me who you are. As for me, my name is Señora Blanca."

When Utuyu showed Señora Blanca Father Juan's piece of paper, she smiled. "Aha!" she said. "So you're Utuyu the singer boy! At last! We've been expecting you. Father Juan asked me just the other day if you'd turned up yet."

"He did?" said Utuyu.

"He most certainly did. And he looked disappointed when I had to tell him that we hadn't seen so much as a hair of your head. But now here you are, and Father Juan will be very happy about it. So what made you decide to come? What is it you want to do?"

"I came because I passed Father Juan's church," said Utuyu. "I remembered he said I couldn't sing in his place if I didn't come here. And he told me you could teach me to speak like the other people speak. That's what I want to do."

"Then you've come to the right place all right," said Señora Blanca. "But you know, learning to speak like the other people isn't easy. You're going to have to learn to read and write as well. It's hard work. You're going to have to keep coming here and coming here, every day you can, until you start to understand what the other people are saying. But if you're ready to work hard, you'll be able to do it."

"That's okay," said Utuyu.

"Lots of the kids come here for a while, and then they go away and don't come back," said Señora Blanca. "They like having a place to come to, and they like the food they get here, and they like playing with the other kids. What they don't like is having to sit still and learn. Are you the kind of boy who can sit still and learn?"

"I can sit still," said Utuyu. "And when I'm sitting still, I sit still better when I have something to do." he said.

Señora Blanca laughed. She was a big woman, and it was a big laugh, such a big laugh that some of the children stopped playing and looked at her to see what she was laughing about. They didn't know what she was laughing about, but her laugh made them laugh, too.

"All right, Utuyu, my small, new friend who knows how to sing," said Señora Blanca, "playtime's almost over now, and we've got to get back to work. You want to stay a while and see what the children do here when they're sitting still?"

Utuyu nodded. He was starting to feel like he'd be happy to stay with this woman with the big laugh any old time.

Señora Blanca clapped her hands, and all the children stopped playing. They went into small rooms and sat in chairs in front of desks.

"You go right in here," said Señora Blanca, taking Utuyu to one of the rooms. "And don't worry. This is the room where everyone begins learning how the other people speak. The kids here don't know much more about it than you do." Then she turned to the children who were already in the room and said, "Listen up everyone, this is Utuyu, and he's come to join us. I want you to make him feel welcome and help him get started. Just because you've already learned a little bit doesn't make you any smarter than he is. What's more, Utuyu can sing like an angel. He's sung all by himself in front of everyone in Father Juan's church!"

All the children stared at Utuyu and looked surprised. He quickly sat down at one of the empty desks.

At the front of the room there was a woman who was talking and making marks on a big green board. Utuyu didn't understand what the marks were for, or why the woman wanted everyone to copy them into the books they had. The funny marks all seemed to have different names you were supposed to say out loud. The names didn't sound like any sounds he'd ever heard before, but Utuyu went ahead and tried to say them anyway.

He was still trying to say them when someone came up behind him and tapped him on the shoulder. Utuyu turned around. It was a tall girl, and she was carrying a book like the other children had. She smiled at Utuyu and put the book on the desk in front of him, along with a pencil. She pointed at the green board, and then at the pencil, and then at the book, and then she went out of the room. From then on, besides trying to say the names of the marks on the green board, Utuyu tried to copy them into his book the way the other children were doing.

That first day in Señora Blanca's school was strange for Utuyu, but it helped that the other children were friendly, and many of them could speak his own language. The girl who had brought him the book and the pencil was particularly helpful. She was much older than the rest of the children, and she seemed to go around being helpful to everyone. When it was time to eat that first day, she came right up to Utuyu with a smile and motioned to him to follow her.

"Where are we going?" Utuyu asked, but the girl pointed to her ears, and then to her mouth, and shook her head. Utuyu frowned at her, but the girl still didn't say anything. She motioned again for Utuyu to follow her, so he did. He followed her to where the food was, and the girl showed him what to do and made sure he got some of everything there was to eat that day. She never said a word and seemed to do all her talking with her hands.

Utuyu learned that the girl's name was Maria Elena and that she'd been at the school for a long time. She didn't speak Utuyu's language, and she didn't speak the language the other people spoke. In fact, Maria Elena couldn't speak at all, and she couldn't hear what people were saying, either. Everyone seemed to understand Maria Elena, though, because of the looks on her face and the gestures she made. Maria Elena seemed to understand what the children were trying to say to her as well.

When it was time for everyone to leave, Señora Blanca waved at Utuyu to come into the room where she was sitting.

"So what do you think?" she asked Utuyu. "You going to come back to us again?"

Utuyu nodded. "I'll come back," he said.

"Good," said Señora Blanca. "One day I want you to tell me how you got to the city in the first place. I'll bet you've had lots of adventures."

Utuyu nodded again.

"Well, being with us is going to be another adventure, and I hope it lasts a long time. You've come a long way from wherever you started. I'm sure it hasn't been any easier for you than for the other kids."

"It's been okay, I guess," Utuyu said. "How long is it going to take me to learn the new language?" he asked.

"Not very long, you'll see," said Señora Blanca. "That is, so long as you keep coming back to us. That's up to you. No one's going to make you come back if you don't want to."

Utuyu didn't know why Señora Blanca thought he wouldn't want to come back, but there were still lots of things he didn't know about yet. There are always lots of things we don't know about, no matter how much we grow. That goes on being true long after we've stopped growing on the outside.

"Tell Father Juan I was here, okay?" Utuyu said to Señora Blanca.

"Of course I will," Señora Blanca said. "I'd tell him anyway, but one of the reasons I'm going to tell him is that I want you to sing in his church again so that one of these days I can come hear you."

By the time Utuyu got back to his room with the tin roof, he had a lot of new things to think about. Every one of those new things he thought about felt good. When he lay on his back on his mattress and looked up at the balloons that night, he tried to say aloud the names of some of the marks he'd copied off the green board into his book.

"A," he said. "B," he said. "C," he said. He didn't get any further, because he couldn't remember how. Besides, before he'd said the sounds three times, I'll bet you can guess what happened. That's right, Utuyu fell asleep.

Chapter Twenty-One

It was not long after that first day at Señora Blanca's school that Utuyu woke up wide awake in the middle of the night. He'd never woken up that way before that he could remember, and he wondered why he'd woken up that way this time. He could tell it was much too early to get up. Some days, Utuyu would wake up when it was still dark, because he'd hear the man coming to take away everyone's bags of garbage. The man walked ahead of the garbage truck, and he'd let the people know the truck was coming by hitting a metal triangle on a string with a metal stick. The sound he made was like a little bell ringing in the darkness. Then, Utuyu would hear the motor of the truck coming along behind. Whenever Utuyu heard the sound of the garbage man coming, he'd know that soon it would be getting light outside.

But this night, when Utuyu suddenly woke up wide-awake, there was no sound of the garbage man coming. There was no sound of anything. Utuyu could feel that it was still going to be dark for a long time. Everything was quiet, as if everyone in the whole city of Oaxaca was still sleeping, and even the garbage man hadn't gotten out of bed yet.

Utuyu turned over on his other side and tried to go back to sleep, but it didn't work. He was too wide-awake, and the most wide-awake parts of him were his ears.

They seemed to be reaching out through the darkness, checking around to see what was going on, doing what his eyes couldn't do at night. Utuyu sat up on his mattress, his arms around his knees, and let both his ears listen. Sure enough, after a moment of listening, his ears heard somebody say something somewhere outside his room. Utuyu couldn't hear what the voice said, but he could tell that whoever's voice it was, that person didn't want him to hear anything at all.

Now what was he supposed to do? He could pretend he hadn't heard anything, but that's hard when you *have* heard something in the middle of the night, and you wonder what it is. He could tell himself that whatever he'd heard didn't matter, and that it would go away. But that's hard, too, when whatever you've heard scares you, and there's no one else around. Telling yourself you're not scared when you *are* scared doesn't help at all. When you're scared, you're scared, and that's all there is to it. And Utuyu was scared.

He thought about crawling behind one of the piles of pieces of old cars and pretending he wasn't there. The trouble with that plan was that he *was* there, and there was nothing he could do about it. What's more, he knew he was supposed to be there for a moment just like this, when something strange was happening at night and no one else was around. The balloon man had said he was supposed to make noise and stuff to let people know that at least *he* was around at night, but Utuyu didn't feel at all like letting whoever it was outside his room know that he was there.

But what else could he do? Scared though he was, Utuyu let out a big noisy yawn. He wished there had been a light that worked that he could turn on, but there wasn't one. He got up off his mattress and started humming to himself. He picked up a piece of an old car and banged it on another piece. Then he stood still and quiet to see what he could hear. He couldn't hear a thing. The voice outside had stopped talking.

Maybe they've gone away, Utuyu thought. He went over to the doorway, and standing in the darkness of his room so no one could see him, he carefully peeked outside. At first he didn't think anyone was there, but then in the shadows under the lights around the flat space, he saw somebody move. In fact, he saw two somebodies standing there together. And then he saw part of a third somebody looking over the top of the wall at the far end of the flat space. As Utuyu stood watching, one of the people in the shadows ran towards him and hid behind one of the cars that were there. Utuyu could tell it was a kid, not a grownup, and he felt a little bit better. But not a whole lot. Something strange was going on, and he was still there all by himself.

Utuyu went back into his room and banged around some more. He wondered if the kid behind the car had come any closer. Maybe the kid would go away, Utuyu thought, if he pretended there was more than one person in the room. He picked the first name that came to his mind and shouted, "Hey, Gabriel, you getting hungry yet?" Of course there was no one in the room to answer, so Utuyu started singing instead, singing and banging around some more. He decided to go take another peek outside to see what was happening now, but when he turned to the doorway, he got a real fright. Someone was standing there, like a black shadow, right there in the doorway of his room.

For a moment, that's the way it was—Utuyu standing still in the darkness, scared right down to his bones, and the shadowy someone in the doorway standing still as well. Then the shadow in the doorway said, "Sky Boy? Is that you in there?"

That was a surprise—someone in the middle of the night knowing his name and talking his own language. "Who are you?" Utuyu said in a small voice.

"What do you mean who am I?" said the voice. "You just asked me if I was hungry! You crazy or something?"

Yes, it was Gabriel, all right. Then Gabriel said, "What are you doing here, anyway? Nobody's ever here."

"I live here," Utuyu said. "I look after the balloons."

"Well, how about that!" said Gabriel. Then he turned, gave a whistle, and motioned to someone else outside to come. Two other kids came to the door. "It's okay," Gabriel told them. "We're in luck. It's only a little guy in here, and he's a friend of mine."

Utuyu wasn't sure about the "friend" part of what Gabriel said. Friends didn't go creeping around in the middle of the night like this. Friends didn't scare each other the way Utuyu had been scared. In fact, friends didn't act the way Gabriel had been acting at all.

"What are you guys doing here, anyway?" Utuyu asked.

"It's like this, Sky Boy," Gabriel said. "I found this place a while ago, and I figured there were so many balloons here that no one would notice if a bunch or two were missing. So me and my buddies here help ourselves to a couple of bunches from time to time. Hey, look," said Gabriel pointing to the ceiling of Utuyu's room. "Don't tell me there aren't enough balloons here to go around!"

"What do you do with the balloons after?" asked Utuyu.

"We sell them, of course, dummy. What do you think?" Gabriel answered. "Not in the big square, though. We sell them down by the market. No one else sells balloons down there."

Utuyu thought about that. Here was Gabriel calling him a dummy again, and he didn't like that. He didn't say anything, though.

"Now that you're here," Gabriel went on, "it's going to be a whole lot easier. Now we won't have to worry about getting caught."

"What about me?" asked Utuyu.

"What do you mean what about you?"

"What am I supposed to say to the man when some of his balloons aren't here when the people come to get them?" Utuyu said.

"You just tell the man someone must have forgotten to bring their balloons back," said Gabriel.

All sorts of thoughts were running around in Utuyu's head. On the one hand, he didn't want to say no to Gabriel. Gabriel might not be a friend exactly, but he was someone Utuyu had known for a while, someone who seemed to know how things worked in Oaxaca. He didn't want Gabriel to go on thinking he was a dummy, either.

On the other hand, he knew Gabriel's plan wouldn't work. Nobody forgot to bring their balloons back at night. If they did forget, why would they come to get their balloons again in the morning?

There was something else that bothered Utuyu, too. He was supposed to be there to keep the balloons safe, and if he didn't keep them safe, the man would probably kick him out of his room and find someone else to look after the balloons. Then he'd have to start looking for somewhere to live all over again.

As Utuyu was thinking about all these things, he had a bad feeling inside. It was just a feeling, not a real thought that he could think about or talk about. He remembered the first night he'd spent in Oaxaca, sleeping in the doorway with the man and his little boy. When Utuyu had gone to sleep that night, he'd had a yellow balloon tied to his wrist. When he'd woken up, the man and the boy were gone, and so was his balloon. He'd felt bad inside that someone had taken his balloon, and he had that same bad feeling now. He wished Gabriel had never shown up.

"So what do you say, Sky Boy?" said Gabriel. "We got a deal?"

This was one deal that Utuyu didn't feel good about. He shook his head.

"What's that supposed to mean?" said Gabriel. "What's the matter with you?"

"You're going to get me in trouble," said Utuyu. "Nobody forgets to bring their balloons. That's a dumb idea." Utuyu hadn't meant to say the word "dumb," but when he'd said it, he felt better. He felt that for once he knew how things worked in Oaxaca better than Gabriel did.

"So you think up something else," said Gabriel.

"Why am I supposed to think up something else so that you guys can take balloons and sell them down at the market?" said Utuyu. That felt like a good question to Utuyu, particularly when Gabriel didn't seem to have an answer for it.

Gabriel turned to the other kids. For a moment the three of them talked in low voices so that Utuyu couldn't hear what they were saying. Then Gabriel said, "I'll tell you what we'll do. My buddies have agreed that we'll give you some of the money we make when we sell the balloons. You don't have to do anything. How about that?"

That made Utuyu think again. If the balloon man went on giving him money just for sleeping there, and now if Gabriel wanted to give him more money for doing nothing at all, and on top of that, if he went on making money by himself singing to people in the big square, then he was going to have a lot of money to put in the tin box. He might need a second box before long.

That was a good thought, but bad thoughts followed right after it. Suppose the balloon man kicked him out when he found some balloons were missing? Then, thought Utuyu, he wouldn't be getting any money from the balloon man anymore, and he wouldn't get any money from Gabriel, and he wouldn't have a place to live, and if he didn't have a place to live, he might not be able to go to Señora Blanca's school anymore. If that happened, he wouldn't be able to sing in Father Juan's church.

"No," Utuyu said to Gabriel. "I like the way things are now. Go get your balloons somewhere else."

Gabriel looked surprised, like he hadn't expected Utuyu to say such a thing.

"You owe me, you know, Sky Boy," said Gabriel. "Who was it who got you into the back of the truck when you were coming to Oaxaca?"

"You did," said Utuyu.

"Who was it who stopped you getting squashed like a banana when you got here?" asked Gabriel.

"You did," said Utuyu.

"Who was it who kept an eye on you and told you how things worked here?" asked Gabriel.

"You did. Sort of," said Utuyu.

"What do you mean, sort of?" asked Gabriel. "If it wasn't for me, Sky Boy, you wouldn't have lasted here for two seconds."

That made Utuyu feel mad, because he knew it wasn't true.

"I found out how to sing to the people all by myself!" said Utuyu. "I found a place to live all by myself! I found how to get food and stuff all by myself! I found out how to sing in Father Juan's church all by myself!"

"You've met Father Juan?" said Gabriel, and he looked surprised again. "Don't forget I was the one who told you about Father Juan in the first place."

"Yeah, but I met him all by myself!" said Utuyu. "And I found out how to go to Señora Blanca's school all by myself! So there!"

"You're going to school at Señora Blanca's place?" said Gabriel, and he looked more surprised than he had before.

"And I'm going to keep on going there until I can talk like the other people," said Utuyu, feeling madder still, "and if you don't leave me alone with your dumb ideas, I'm going to tell Señora Blanca, and I'll tell Father Juan, too, that you're sneaking around in the middle of the night taking other people's balloons and selling them in the market!"

"Hey, Sky Boy, relax!" said Gabriel. "Okay, okay, so maybe it wasn't such a good idea. But I wouldn't say anything about it to Father Juan and Señora Blanca, if I were you. It's got nothing to do with them. We'll just keep it between you and me, okay?"

Utuyu nodded. Then he said, "Now go away and leave me alone." And that's what Gabriel and his buddies did.

Utuyu tried to go back to sleep, but he couldn't. He was still awake when he heard the sound of the garbage man coming, making the bell sound with his metal triangle. He was still awake when daylight began to brighten the sky. He hadn't had so much as another wink of sleep when the balloon man came to open up his wooden box to sit in by the street.

"Everything go all right last night?" the balloon man asked Utuyu when he saw him sitting in the sun outside his room. "No problems?"

"Everything didn't go all right," said Utuyu. "Some kids came and tried to take some balloons."

"They did?" said the balloon man. "So what happened?"

"They didn't know I was there until I made some noises and stuff," said Utuyu.

"So that's where some of my balloons have been going!" said the balloon man. "What happened then?"

"I told them I was living here to look after the balloons, and to go away and not come back again," said Utuyu. "And then they went away."

The balloon man looked pleased. "I knew you were a good kid," he said, "but until now I didn't know how really good a kid you were. Were you scared?"

"Kind of," Utuyu said.

"You know what?" said the balloon man. "You've just gone and earned yourself a raise. I'm going to pay you a little more than I've been paying you so far. How about that?"

That was fine by Utuyu. What he didn't tell the balloon man, though, was that he'd known who one of the kids was.

Whenever Utuyu bumped into Gabriel after that, which he did from time to time when he went to sing in the big square, Gabriel looked at him differently. Gabriel talked to him differently, too. For instance, Gabriel never called him a dummy again.

Chapter Twenty-Two

Utuyu hardly missed a day at Señora Blanca's school. There were children there who had been coming to the school for a long time before Utuyu got there, but they didn't come every day. One day they'd be there, and the next day they wouldn't. Some just disappeared and didn't come anymore at all. There were often new faces that came and went before Utuyu had a chance to learn the names that went with them.

When one of the children who had been there a long time stopped coming, Señora Blanca sometimes knew why. One child might have had to go back to work at her home in the mountains. Another might have found work to do somewhere in the city, the way Utuyu had found work looking after the balloons. If their work happened at the same times that the school was open, they couldn't be in two places at once. Most of the time, though, nobody knew why a child stopped coming to the school.

But when Maria Elena stopped coming to the school, first one day and then day after day, *everyone* wanted to know where she had gone. All Señora Blanca said was that Maria Elena had had an accident. Someone had hurt her, and she had to stay home now. She might come back sometime when she felt better, Señora Blanca said, but in all the time that Utuyu was at the school, he never saw Maria Elena again.

As Utuyu watched children come and then not come anymore, he came to feel that all sorts of things could happen to stop a child coming to the school. He hoped none of those things, whatever they were, would happen to him. Señora Blanca's school was the place he liked to go more than anywhere else. When Señora Blanca began asking him to do some of the things Maria Elena had done before, like putting things away and keeping them in their right places, or helping to clean up the tables after the children had eaten, he felt especially happy. He didn't like the days when the school was closed for some reason or another and he had to wait for it to open again.

It didn't take long for Utuyu to learn to say all the letters of the new language in order, or to write them in his book. After that, be began to learn how you put two or three of them together to make little words like "yes" and "no." Then he learned longer words like "hello" and "good bye." Once he'd learned how to say them out loud, he began to say them to the people in the big square when he went up to their tables to sing. When the people said the words back to him, and he knew what the people were saying, Utuyu felt like something wonderful was happening.

There were still people in the big square, though, who didn't seem to understand anything he said. Utuyu couldn't understand anything they said to him, either. These were usually the people with faces that were as white as the moon. Utuyu didn't know what kind of sounds these people would make when they opened their mouths. He thought that maybe they should go to Señora Blanca's school, too.

One day, when all the children were leaving, and Utuyu was helping put everything back where it belonged so it would be ready for the next day, he asked Señora Blanca about the people with the white faces. Señora

Blanca took Utuyu to a wall with pictures hanging on it. One picture looked like a blue and green plate on a black tablecloth.

"This is a picture of where we all live," she said, "only it's really round like a ball, and there's sky all around it. Nobody lives in the blue parts. They're all water. But people live almost everywhere else, and they come in lots of different shapes and colors and sizes. They have lots of different ways of talking, too." Señora Blanca asked Utuyu if he remembered that he'd once lived in a place where even people who lived nearby couldn't understand each other. Utuyu remembered that very well from his long walk to the city.

That night, Utuyu lay on his mattress, looking up at the ceiling covered with balloons. He thought about what Señora Blanca had said. How could people live on a ball in the sky, he wondered? It would be like trying to live on a balloon, he thought. Even if the balloon was a really big one, big enough for lots of people to stand on, some of the people would have to fall off.

Señora Blanca can't be right, Utuyu thought. *I'd know it if I was walking around on a ball in the sky.*

Can you understand how Utuyu felt? It's hard to imagine that that's what we're all doing—walking around on a ball in the sky. It's hard to understand why we don't fall off, or why some of the people who live on the bottom side of the ball aren't walking around upside down. Utuyu was learning a lot of things at Señora Blanca's school, but it would still be a long time before he understood things like that. It probably took you a long time, too.

Utuyu went on singing at Father Juan's church whenever it was the first quiet day after the moon had become full. He learned to sing some of the church songs in the new language he was learning at Señora Blanca's school. The people seemed to like these songs when he sang them in the church, so he tried singing them to the people sitting at the tables in the big square. Utuyu thought these new songs sounded sad, but he sang them anyway, because he liked singing in the new language.

Some of the people at the tables seemed to like the new songs, and some of the people didn't seem to like them so much. At first, Utuyu found it hard to guess which people would like them and which people wouldn't. Older people, it seemed, were more likely to like the songs than younger people, so he sang them most at tables where there were people with old faces and grey hair. It seemed to work, because they always gave Utuyu money. Maybe it was something to do with why so many of the people in the church were old people, too.

Father Juan began asking Utuyu to stay a while after the people left the church. When Father Juan first asked him, Utuyu thought it was because Father Juan wanted him to help put things away, like he did at the school. That wasn't it, though. Father Juan wanted to tell him stories. They'd sit on the edge of the fountain, and Father Juan always had a new story to tell. Utuyu liked having Father Juan tell him stories, even though most of the stories Father Juan told him were about people who did bad things and got punished. In lots of the stories, people died. Utuyu listened without saying anything. He was afraid Father Juan would stop telling him any stories at all if he said he didn't like some of them. When the stories were short and simple ones, Father Juan would tell them slowly in the new language. Utuyu learned a lot of new words this way.

Some of the stories were about the people who were statues in the church, or about the people in the sad pictures on the walls. When Father Juan was telling Utuyu a story like that, they'd go inside the church, and Father Juan would show him who was in the story and what part of the story was happening in the pictures.

Father Juan said all the stories were true stories, but Utuyu didn't think they could be. He didn't say anything about that to Father Juan, though. Father Juan told lots of stories about a man who he said could make more food happen when there wasn't enough, or who could tell a dead person to get up and walk and make it happen. Utuyu had never seen anyone do things like that. If anyone could, he thought, they'd be doing it all the time. As for the pictures in the church, Utuyu didn't think there were really people with wings flying about anywhere, or that you could really sit on a cloud in the sky, although that seemed a little easier to believe.

One day, Father Juan asked Utuyu if he'd like to have a different name. Utuyu thought that was a strange question. Wasn't one name enough for one person? When he asked Father Juan what he'd want another name for, Father Juan said that now that Utuyu was learning to speak the new language, he might like to have a name more like the names people had who spoke the new language. Utuyu didn't know right then whether he felt having a new name was a good idea. It might be, and then again it might not be. He'd always been Utuyu, and there was something that didn't feel good about suddenly becoming someone else. He liked being who he was.

"Think about it," Father Juan said. "But if you decide you want a new name, I can't give it to you just like that. There are some things you'll have to learn before I can give it to you."

"Things like what?" Utuyu asked.

"Like why the people come to this church and why they say the things they are saying," said Father Juan. "You'll have to learn to believe that what they are saying is true. Then I can give you a new name."

Father Juan was speaking Utuyu's own language right then, but all the same, Utuyu didn't understand what he meant by learning to believe something was true. It seemed to him that a person already knew if something was true or not. If someone told you it was raining when the sun was shining, you knew what they said wasn't true. If someone told you that last night the moon had been full when you'd seen for yourself that it was still small and growing in the sky, they were just making up a story. And if someone told you that tomorrow something would happen that hadn't happened yet, then they were just guessing, weren't they?

Utuyu tried, but he couldn't figure out what Father Juan meant. What's more, he couldn't figure out why he should try to figure out what Father Juan meant. Getting a new name didn't seem like a good reason to try to figure it all out, because the name "Utuyu" was already his, and he liked it, and it worked just fine.

Utuyu didn't want to make Father Juan mad, though, so all he said was, "I'll think about it."

Chapter Twenty-Three

The nights of the full moons came and went. Each time they did, Utuyu waited for the next quiet day. When it came, he'd go to Father Juan's church and sing. He'd learned now that the quiet day was called Sunday, and if he wanted to know ahead of time when it would be coming, he could ask anyone, anyone at all in the streets, and they would tell him, in the new language, "Tomorrow," or "The day after tomorrow." He didn't have to guess by the sun anymore what time it was, either. That was something else Utuyu could ask people. They would look at the watch on their wrist and tell him, and Utuyu knew what they were saying and understood what it meant. He didn't really understand how you could measure the days in numbers, or how it happened that the sun seemed to know where it should be when the hands of the clock in the big church in the square were in a certain place. He didn't know how the sun worked, but he knew it couldn't have a watch—not to mention a wrist to put a watch on.

One day I'm going to have a watch to put on my wrist, he thought. *And when I do, people will be able to ask* me *what time it is and not the other way around.*

Utuyu kept on looking after the balloons at night and going to Señora Blanca's school in the daytime. Soon, he'd been going to the school longer than almost any of the other children, and then, after a while, he'd been going there longest of all. When he was at the school now, he talked only in the new language, just the way Señora Blanca and the other teachers did when they were talking together. Utuyu understood what they were saying, even when they weren't talking to him.

That was how Utuyu got his first hint that once again something was about to change in his life. Señora Blanca and one of the teachers were talking together in Señora Blanca's room, but the door was open. Utuyu heard the teacher say, "Yes, I agree. Utuyu is ready to go now."

Señora Blanca said, "I'll be sorry to see him go." And the teacher said, "I will be, too."

Nobody said anything to him, though—not that day or for many days after. That was hard for Utuyu, because he knew from what he had heard that a change was coming, but he didn't know exactly what the change was, and he didn't know when it was going to happen. He wondered about it a lot. He wondered about it when he was doing his work at school, and he wondered about it when he was lying on his mattress looking up at the balloons on the ceiling of his room.

When a balloon had words written on it, as some of them did, Utuyu could read those words now. Lying there wondering what was going to happen to him and when, Utuyu read one balloon that said, "Happy Birthday!" and another that said "Congratulations!" The balloons had happy faces on them as well as the words, but Utuyu didn't feel happy. He didn't feel sad, though, either. What he felt was uncertain. He felt uncertain about how he was supposed to be feeling, because he didn't know what it was that he was supposed to have feelings about. He wished someone would say something about what was going to happen to him and when it was going to happen, because then he'd know how to feel about it.

At last Señora Blanca *did* say something. One day at school, she put her arm around Utuyu and said, "Come with me." She took Utuyu into her room, and when they were sitting there together, she said, "Remember the first time we saw each other? There you were, standing outside the big doors. You looked very small out there then."

Utuyu remembered that moment very well. "You looked very big, Señora," he said.

"Well, you don't look so small to me anymore, my not-too-little friend," Señora Blanca said. "Just look! Your feet are touching the floor now!"

They *were* touching the floor. Utuyu couldn't swing them back and forth the way he used to.

Without thinking about it, Utuyu said, "What's going to happen to me?"

"Ah, so you've already guessed," said Señora Blanca. "So now I'll tell you."

Utuyu didn't say that he hadn't guessed anything, that he'd heard about it through the open door.

What Señora Blanca told Utuyu was that the time had come for him to go off to a school like the schools where the other children went who spoke the new language.

"You can talk like them now," Señora Blanca said, "and you've learned about letters and words and numbers, as well as lots of other things. But there's so much more for you to learn! Here, we can't teach you all those things you're going to need to know. Somebody else has to do that."

"So I have to go away," said Utuyu. He remembered the time when he'd been living at Ita's house in The Mountains to the North, and one day Ita had told him he had to go away to the city. Would it always be like this, Utuyu wondered? Would someone always be telling him he had to go away?

"No," said Señora Blanca, "you don't have to go away. What you have to do is go on growing, just the way you've been growing all the time you've been here. Here at the school, we're like a pair of shoes that have become too small for you. You need a bigger pair so that your feet can have room to go on growing the way they're supposed to."

Instead of making Utuyu feel good about what was going to happen, what Señora Blanca said about the shoes made him feel bad. He knew what happened to old shoes that were too small. They got given away, or thrown away, and you never saw them again.

"What's the matter, Utuyu?" Señora Blanca said. She could see from the look on Utuyu's face that he was worried about something.

"I don't want never to see you again," Utuyu said. "Like old shoes."

"You're right," said Señora Blanca. "We're not really like old shoes at all. We're more like shoes that are always new and ready for new feet to get into them for a time. And then those feet get bigger and step into bigger shoes that are waiting for them. The smaller shoes don't go anywhere. They just wait for other, smaller feet to come along and get in."

It was hard for Utuyu to imagine all these feet getting in and out of shoes, but something about what Señora Blanca said made him feel a little better.

"How about this?" Señora Blanca said. "Let's say we're like the pair of pants you're wearing. It's time to add some more cloth to the bottom of the legs to make the legs longer. It's time to make your pants bigger around the waist, so that you can go on wearing the same pants and go on getting bigger at the same time."

Making his old pants longer and bigger was easier for Utuyu to imagine, and he liked the idea a lot better. But he didn't feel better for long, though, because then Señora Blanca said, "And we've found you a place to live near the school."

Now that was something Utuyu hadn't expected to hear at all. A new place to live? Why? He didn't need a new place to live, and, what's more, he didn't want a new place to live. He wanted to go on living just the way he was living, sleeping on his old, familiar mattress at night and looking after the balloons.

"I don't want to live somewhere new," Utuyu told Señora Blanca. "I like where I'm living now, and I want to go on living there!"

"I understand," Señora Blanca said. "Of course you do. But if you're going to go to the new school and learn new things, you're going to have to have a proper place to live. The people who run the new school don't want their students living by themselves on the street."

"There's nothing wrong with the place I live, and I don't live on the street," said Utuyu. "I live in a place of my own, and I want to go on living there!"

"It would take a lot of time for you to walk to the new school," Señora Blanca said.

"I don't mind walking," said Utuyu.

"There'll be a lot of work for you to do at the new school, and when you get home from the new school, there will be more work for you to do to get ready for the next day."

"I don't mind working," said Utuyu.

"You'll need someone to help you with the work," Señora Blanca said. "And you'll need someone to make sure you have food, and clean clothes, and that you get up at the right time, and get to the school at the right time."

"I can already do those things by myself," said Utuyu.

"Yes, you can," Señora Blanca said. "But now there will be too much for you to do all by yourself, and you're going to need someone to help you."

"I don't need someone to help me," said Utuyu, "and I want to go on living where I'm living now."

Señora Blanca sat back in her chair and looked at Utuyu. "I know how you feel," she said, but Utuyu didn't think Señora Blanca knew how he felt at all. If she knew how he felt, she wouldn't go on telling him he couldn't go on living where he lived anymore, would she?

For a few moments, neither Señora Blanca nor Utuyu said anything more to each other. Utuyu looked down at his shoes, and then up at Señora Blanca, and then down at his shoes again. When he looked up at Señora Blanca once more, she seemed to be waiting for him to say something.

"I'm going to go on living where I am," he said, very quietly.

"You can't, Utuyu," said Señora Blanca, just as quietly. "I'm sorry, but you can't do that."

Yes, I can, too! Utuyu thought to himself. *I can live where I want to, and I can do what I want to, and no one can make me do anything I don't want to, and I don't want to live somewhere different!*

"I won't go to the new school!" Utuyu said. He didn't know what more to say, so he got out of his chair, and he walked out of Señora Blanca's room, and then he ran past the other children, and he ran right out of the big doors and into the street, and he ran all the way back to where he lived, right past the man in his wooden box without saying hello, and right into his room where he lived. He sat down in the furthest, darkest corner of his room and crossed his arms across his chest.

"I'm going to stay right here!" he said. He said it right out loud. And then he said, out louder still, "And nobody's going to make me leave here! So there!"

Utuyu didn't feel like going back to Señora Blanca's school the next day, so he didn't. Or the next day. Or the next day after that.

Chapter Twenty-Four

When the balloon man came the following morning, Utuyu stayed in his room. He stayed in his room while the balloon man sat in his wooden box and drank out of his plastic cup. He stayed in his room while the people came with their cars and left them there for the day. He stayed in his room while the people came to pick up their balloons and take them to the big square. He still hadn't come out of his room by the time the sun was high in the sky and the day was hot. He lay on his mattress and stared at the ceiling, thinking about what was going on at Señora Blanca's school while he wasn't there.

Everyone will be wondering where I am, Utuyu thought, and that thought felt good. *I don't have to go there if I don't want to,* he said to himself. *I don't have to do anything I don't want to do.*

Utuyu was right. There wasn't anyone around who could make him do anything at all. He could eat whenever he wanted to, and whatever he wanted to, or he could decide not to eat at all. He could walk around the city in any direction he wanted to go and for as long as he liked, or he could stay in his room all day. He could sing to the people in the big square if he felt like it, and if he didn't feel like it, he didn't have to sing to anyone, ever. He didn't have to talk to anyone if he didn't want to. He could stay all by himself for as long as he liked, thinking his own thoughts, and doing whatever he wanted to do, or not doing anything.

Utuyu was thinking about whether he felt like doing something for the rest of the day, when the balloon man came to his door and looked in.

"You in there, kid?" the balloon man asked.

"Yes," said Utuyu.

"What are you doing in there?" the balloon man asked.

"Nothing," Utuyu said.

"You feeling okay?" the balloon man asked.

"Yup," said Utuyu.

"You're not sick or something?" the balloon man said.

"Nope," said Utuyu.

"That's good," said the balloon man. "I was wondering. Say, aren't you supposed to be in school today?"

"I don't have to go there if I don't want to," Utuyu said, "and I didn't want to go there today."

"I know what you mean," said the balloon man. "There are days like that."

"I'm not going to go there anymore at all," Utuyu said.

"Well now, that's something different," said the balloon man. "What are you going to do instead?"

"Whatever I want," said Utuyu.

"That's nothing new," said the balloon man. "That's what you've been doing every day already, isn't it?"

Utuyu thought about that. Then he said, "Yup. And that's what I'm going to go on doing."

"You going to ask me to come in?" said the balloon man. "Or are you going to leave me leaning up here against the door?"

"You can come in if you want to," said Utuyu. "You can do anything you want."

The balloon man laughed. "Not me, I can't! I'm not lucky like you with no one to look after. If I could do anything I wanted, I'd be down there somewhere on the beach, laying in a hammock, sipping on a cool drink, and watching the boats go by. That's what I'd be doing."

"So why don't you go do it?" said Utuyu.

"'Cause if I did that, who'd look after my woman?" said the balloon man. "Who'd be around to put food on the table? Where would we get our clothes? All that stuff doesn't grow on trees for the picking, you know. Somebody's got to make it all happen."

"Yeah," said Utuyu, "but you make it happen because you want to make it happen, right? That's what you want to do."

"Some days I do, and some days I don't," said the balloon man. "That's the way it goes. And when the days come along when I don't want to do it, I do it anyway, because if I don't do the things I don't want to do on the days I don't want to do them, there's gonna be nobody else around to do them. Know what I mean?"

Utuyu sort of did know what the balloon man meant and sort of didn't know what he meant.

"So what happened at school?" said the balloon man. "What happened to make you not want to do what you used to want to do? How come you decided to do something else, something else you don't know if you want to do or not, because you don't even know what it is?"

"I do know what it is," said Utuyu, "and I know I don't want to do it. They told me I have to go off to a different school and that I can't live here anymore if I do. That's what."

"Well, how about that!" said the balloon man. "That's a lot for anyone to think about, 'cause maybe it's a bad thing and maybe it isn't. Those kind of things take a lot of thinking about."

Utuyu felt mad. "I've already thought about it!" he shouted. "It's a bad thing and I'm not going to do it!"

"Okay, okay!" said the balloon man. "Take it easy, kid! Turn down the volume! No reason to bust my ear drums!"

But Utuyu didn't feel like taking it easy. "Nobody's going to make me leave this place! It's my place!"

"Well, it sort of is and it sort of isn't," said the balloon man. "It's only your place so long as I let you stay here, right? And it's not my place, either. I only get to work here as long as the guy who owns the place lets me work here, right? Things can change, just like that!" The balloon man snapped his fingers. "And when they change, we gotta change right along with them. That is, unless we want to get left behind, and I don't know about you, kid, but I can tell you I'm not the kind of guy who goes and let's himself get left behind, not if I can help it."

"Who'd look after the balloons if I went and lived somewhere else?" asked Utuyu.

"Who do you think?" said the balloon man. "I'd go find myself another kid. Another kid like you."

When the balloon man said that, Utuyu felt scared. It was like the feeling he'd had that night when he'd woken up in the darkness and heard strange noises outside his room. The sounds had made him feel he wasn't safe anymore, that something awful could be about to happen. He saw a picture in his mind of his room, the very room where he was now, and there was a strange boy living there instead of himself. The strange boy was doing all the things Utuyu was used to doing—talking to the balloon man in his wooden box, watching the cars come in when it was morning and go out in the afternoon, giving the people their bunches of balloons and taking them in again, and in the picture in Utuyu's mind, this strange boy was lying on Utuyu's very own mattress and looking up at the balloons at night the way he did.

If a strange boy is doing all the things I'm used to doing, Utuyu wondered, *what will I be doing instead?* Utuyu couldn't find any picture in his mind to tell him the answer to that big question. Without an answer, that question was not only a big one, but it was a scary one as well.

When the balloon man went back to sit in his box again, Utuyu felt very much alone. He was always alone in his room, but he didn't usually feel alone. Being alone and feeling alone isn't the same thing. You can be alone somewhere, and it can feel good to be all by yourself and away from noisy people. But when you *feel* alone, it's not a good feeling at all. You can feel alone even when there are lots of noisy people all around you. They may all be talking together, and laughing together, and having a good time together, but if you're there, too, and nobody notices you're there, or seems to care if you're there or not, it can feel awful. Feeling that way is called feeling "lonely." Lonely is exactly how Utuyu felt when the balloon man said that if Utuyu wasn't there anymore to look after the balloons, he'd go find another kid. Utuyu felt the balloon man didn't really care if he was there or not.

Utuyu's lonely feeling didn't go away. He was still feeling lonely when Sunday came, and it was time for him to go to the house of the woman who sold bread to take a bath. He always felt glad when he went there on Sundays. He liked knowing the woman would always be there, and she always was, and he liked being with her children for a while. When he went to the woman's house on that particular Sunday when he was feeling lonely, though, it didn't feel the same. The woman was busy doing some washing and hardly looked up at him when he came in. Her children were busy playing together and didn't ask him to join in their game. That's the way it often was when Utuyu went to the woman's house, and it had never bothered him before. On that particular Sunday, it bothered him.

When Utuyu had finished taking his bath and had gotten himself dressed, the woman put down her washing and looked at him. She shook her head.

"Those pants are getting too small," she said. "The legs are too short, and look how tight they are around the middle! My, oh my," she said, "it's time for a change again," and she went and got Utuyu a different pair of pants that were bigger.

"So how are things going at school?" she asked, as Utuyu was getting into the different pants.

"I'm not going to school anymore," Utuyu said.

"And why not?" asked the woman. "You think you've learned all there is to know already?"

"They want to send me to another school, and they say I have to go live in another place, and I can't live where I'm living anymore, and I don't want to do it," said Utuyu.

"You do what they tell you!" said the woman. "You're a lucky boy to have a new school to go to, and luckier still to have a place to live no matter where it is! You want to end up on the streets forever like so many of the kids you see around here?"

"I like things the way they are," said Utuyu.

"And just who do you think you are to be deciding how things are going to be?" said the woman. "Nobody gets to decide that! All you get to do is make the best you can out of what happens, and don't ever forget it."

"I wouldn't be able to come here anymore," said Utuyu.

"And just how long did you think you were going to come here, and use my soap and water, and get my children's clothes? Until you were an old man?"

Utuyu didn't have an answer for that, because he'd never thought about it.

"Now come along. I've got bread to sell, and you'd better have some good songs to sing," said the woman.

Utuyu felt the woman didn't care if he was around or not, any more than the balloon man did, and if she didn't care about whether he was there or not, why should he care about helping her sell her bread?

"I don't want to sing today," he said to the woman.

The woman put her hands on her hips and looked down at him with a frown. "In that case, young-man-who-only-wants-to-do-what-he-wants-to-do, you take those pants right off, here and now, and get back into your dirty pants that are too small and too tight. You go right on back to wherever you came from!"

Utuyu hadn't expected to hear anything like that! He looked at the woman frowning down at him, and before he could stop himself, he was crying. The other children stopped playing their game and looked to see what all the fuss was about.

"That's right, go on, cry," she said. "Cry all you want to. But either you come sing, or you can cry your way home in your own pair of dirty old pants."

A lot of children would have done what they were told, but there was something inside Utuyu that was making him feel angry—angry with everything and everybody on that particular Sunday. When you feel angry, the kind of angry Utuyu was feeling right then, it can make you do things you wouldn't do otherwise. That can turn out to be a good thing, and it can turn out to be a bad thing, too. Utuyu didn't know which kind of thing he was doing, but he slowly took off the pants the woman had given him, got back into the pants he'd come with, and without saying anything to anybody, walked out of the woman's house. No one was going to make him sing if he didn't want to. Not anybody. Not even the woman who sold bread.

Chapter Twenty-Five

The days passed, but Utuyu went on feeling mad and lonely. The next Sunday that came along was a Sunday after the full moon, but Utuyu didn't go to Father Juan's church to sing. He stayed in his room all by himself, all day long. If no one in all of Oaxaca cared if he were in Oaxaca or not, then he wasn't going to care about anyone in Oaxaca. So there!

When evening came, and it was beginning to get dark, Utuyu had had enough of feeling mad all by himself. If you want to stay mad at people, you need to have people you can stay mad at. So, Utuyu decided that he'd go and be mad at the people in the big square. He walked through the streets with a big scowl on his face, and every time someone passed him in the streets, he said, out loud, "I don't care about you!"

When he got to the square, he went straight back to the same bench where he'd sat when he was feeling mad before—the time when it didn't seem there was anywhere for him to live in Oaxaca. The big square was the same as it always was. There was the building in the middle with its roof that looked like a hat. People were walking up the steps around the building, and going down the steps that went under the building, just the way they always did.

"I don't care about any of you!" Utuyu said out loud from his bench. Of course the people going up and down the steps were too far away to hear him, but Utuyu felt good saying it anyway.

Grownups and children were walking around the big square, just the way they always did. A man passed by Utuyu's bench with a little boy sitting on his shoulders. "I don't care about you!" Utuyu said as the man passed. The man turned to Utuyu and said, "What?" Utuyu didn't say anything. He just scowled. The man shook his head and went on walking.

A woman and a little girl went by. The little girl was holding her mother's hand with one of her hands and pulling a toy duck on a string with the other hand. The toy duck had wheels on it, but it kept falling over on the rough stones. The little girl kept pulling on her mother's hand for her to stop while she put the duck right way up, but as soon as they started to walk again, the duck fell over again. The mother looked impatient. She stooped over to pick up the duck, and the little girl began to jump up and down and whine.

"I don't care about you!" Utuyu said. The mother and the little girl were too busy with what they were doing to hear him, but that didn't matter to Utuyu. He'd told them how he felt, whether they'd heard him or not.

All the people selling things in the big square were going about their business the way they always did. "I don't care about you!" Utuyu said to all of them at once.

There were people sitting at the tables, eating and drinking, just like always. "I don't care about you!" Utuyu said "And I'm not going to sing to you, either! So there!"

Everything in the big square was the same, but it all looked different to Utuyu. Well, it *looked* the same, but it didn't *feel* the same. To him, it didn't feel friendly or exciting anymore. It felt like someone else's place, a strange place, as strange to him as the very first time he'd seen it. He didn't feel like he belonged there anymore.

There have been times when I've felt like that, and maybe you've felt that way, too. I don't like the feeling at all. It seems to me like looking at the world through a pair of dark sunglasses that make the bright, warm world go darker and colder and seem farther away. The people and the buildings and the trees and the sky all look like they have the same shapes you're used to, but with sunglasses on, they don't feel the same way they usually do. Feelings can do that, too. The same old world feels different when you're looking at it through mad and lonely feelings the way Utuyu was.

Then Utuyu saw someone he didn't feel like being mad at. Sitting on a bench a little way away was one of Ita's children, and it was Nino. For a moment Utuyu forgot he was lonely and mad, and he ran over to where Nino was sitting to say hello.

"We've heard all about you!" Nino said to Utuyu. "You're famous around here for your singing!"

"I don't do that anymore," Utuyu told Nino. "Nobody cares if I sing or not."

"Where are you living?" Nino asked him. "You found a place?"

Before he could answer, Utuyu saw someone else he knew, but this someone else was someone he wasn't sure he was glad to see at all. Father Juan was walking across the square toward him, and he had a serious look on his face. When Father Juan walked up to Utuyu, he said, in the new language, "So there you are! Where have you been?"

"Around," Utuyu answered, also in the new language.

"You and I have some talking to do," Father Juan went on.

"I don't feel like talking to anyone right now," Utuyu said. Seeing Father Juan like that made him remember his lonely, mad feelings again.

"It seems you feel like talking to your friend here," said Father Juan, "and you and I are going to have a talk, whether you feel like talking to me or not. I'm going to sit right over there." Father Juan pointed to another bench. "When you're done talking to your friend, I'll be waiting for you. You save some of that talking you don't want to do for me."

"Who was that?" Nino asked, when Father Juan went over to sit on his bench.

"Oh, someone I know," said Utuyu.

"How did you learn to talk to him in his language," Nino asked.

"I've been going to school," said Utuyu.

"To school?" said Nino. "How did you get into a school?"

"That man told the people to let me in," said Utuyu. "And they did."

"Wow!" said Nino. "That's cool! It must be great to go to a school! You like it?"

"I liked it," said Utuyu, "but I'm not going to a school anymore."

"Why not?" Nino asked.

"They want me to do things I don't want to do," said Utuyu, "and I'm not going to do them. That's why."

"So what are you going to do now?" asked Nino.

"I don't know," said Utuyu, "but I don't like it here in Oaxaca anymore."

"Come back to Ita's house with us," Nino said. "We're all going back there for a while. She's always asking us if we've seen you in Oaxaca."

In all the thinking that Utuyu had done about what he was going to do next, he hadn't thought about going back to Ita's house since the time the machinery moved into the flat space behind the boards where he'd lived. But when he thought about it now, he liked the idea. If no one in Oaxaca cared if he was in Oaxaca or not, why shouldn't he go back to Ita's house for a while? And if Ita was always asking about him, maybe she'd let him stay.

"When are you going Ita's house?" Utuyu asked.

"Tomorrow night," Nino said. "You want to come? There's going to be a big party there the day after tomorrow."

"Sure!" said Utuyu. "I'll come with you!"

"So be here tomorrow when it gets dark," said Nino. "We'll look for you before we go."

For the first time in many days, Utuyu felt good about something. His lonely, mad feelings didn't seem so important anymore. But Father Juan was still sitting on his bench, staring at him. When Nino left, Utuyu thought about walking away without talking to Father Juan at all. Why should he talk to Father Juan if he didn't want to, he asked himself? But when Father Juan gestured to him to come sit beside him on the bench, Utuyu did.

"You didn't come to sing on Sunday," said Father Juan, "and Señora Blanca tells me you haven't shown up at school lately. What's going on?"

Utuyu didn't say anything.

"Let me guess, then," said Father Juan. "You don't want to go to a new school. Right?"

Utuyu nodded.

"And you don't want to live somewhere new," said Father Juan. "Right?"

Utuyu nodded again. He wondered why Father Juan had to ask him so many questions if he already knew all the answers before he asked them.

"I thought so," said Father Juan. "Well," he said, and his face took on a kinder look than it had before, "I don't blame you."

That seemed to be the end of their talk, because neither Father Juan nor Utuyu said anything else for a while.

"Can I go now?" Utuyu asked.

"I guess you can do anything you want," Father Juan said. "I can't make you stay here with me any more than

I, or Señora Blanca, or anyone else, can make you go to the new school or live somewhere new. It's up to you. But I'd like it if you'd stay here just another minute," Father Juan went on. "There's something I'd like to tell you."

"What?" Utuyu asked.

"As a matter of fact, there are *two* things I want to tell you before we say goodbye," said Father Juan. "The first is very simple, and if you think about it, I think you'll find you already know it. It's this: Before you throw something away, it's a good idea to know what it is. Otherwise, you might find you've thrown away something by mistake, something you wanted to keep."

That made sense to Utuyu, but he didn't understand what it had to do with anything that was going on.

"Do you know what I'm saying?" asked Father Juan.

Utuyu did, and at the same time he didn't, so he shrugged his shoulders.

"What I'm saying," said Father Juan, "is that when there's a chance to do something new, something you don't know if you'll like or not because you've never done it before, it's a good idea to try it for a while before you decide it's something you don't want to do. If you don't try something new, how can you ever know whether you might like it or not? You might just throw it away by mistake."

Utuyu thought about that.

"It's like if I gave you a present all wrapped up in paper so you couldn't tell what it was," said Father Juan. "Wouldn't you want to open it before you decided whether to throw it away or not?"

"Sure," said Utuyu, because that was an easy question anyone could answer.

"So why not try out the new school and the new place to live for a while before you decide you don't want them?" said Father Juan.

That was a hard question for Utuyu to answer. In fact, he couldn't find an answer for it—at least not an answer that he liked—so he said, "I want things to stay the way they are."

"They won't," said Father Juan. "They never do. Making things stay the way they are is something nobody can make happen. Not me. Not you. Not Señora Blanca. Not anyone. All we can do is try to help each other while things go on changing around us."

Then Father Juan said, "That's the second thing I wanted to tell you. There are people here who care very much about what happens to you, and who want to help you as things change, which, like I said, they're going to do whether any of us like it or not. I'm one of those people who care about you. Señora Blanca is another. I just wanted you to know that."

Were there really people in Oaxaca who cared about him after all, Utuyu wondered? No matter what Father Juan said, Utuyu still didn't feel sure about it.

"I'm going back to Ita's house in the mountains," was all he could think of to say.

"When?" asked Father Juan.

"Tomorrow," said Utuyu.

"It seems you've made up your mind," said Father Juan.

Utuyu nodded. "I don't like it here in Oaxaca anymore," he said.

"Well then, my young friend," said Father Juan, "I guess it really is time for us to say goodbye to each other."

Utuyu nodded again.

"I wish you good luck," said Father Juan. "I hope you'll find what you're looking for. But don't look for ways to make things to stay the same. That's a waste of time, because staying the same is something things never do."

"Okay," said Utuyu. He was glad this talk seemed to be coming to an end.

"And if you never come back to Oaxaca again," said Father Juan, "and we never see each other again, think of me sometimes, and I'll think of you."

Father Juan got up from the bench and held out his hand. It was a big hand, and when Utuyu put his own hand inside it, his hand felt very small. Then, when he'd let go of Utuyu's hand, Father Juan made the up-and-down and side-to-side gesture Utuyu had seen him make so many times in front of the people in his church.

"God bless you and keep you safe," said Father Juan, and he walked off into the night.

Utuyu felt a little pinch of sadness watching Father Juan go, but then he hopped off the bench to go find the balloon man. He'd better tell him right away that he was going to have to find some other kid to guard his balloons.

Chapter Twenty-Six

Imagine taking a flat sheet of newspaper, one of the big sheets that opens up like a book, and scrumpling it up as much as you can. I mean, scrumpling it *really* hard, and maybe pounding on it a bit, too. If you did that, the sheet of newspaper wouldn't end up looking much like a sheet of newspaper anymore, would it? Instead of being flat like it was before you started all your scrumpling and pounding, now it would have more folds and creases and pointy pieces and dents than you could count. It wouldn't look much like a sheet of newspaper anymore, but it would look a lot like the shape of The Mountains to the North. That is, if you were a bird flying as high in the sky as a bird can fly, and you were looking down on The Mountains to the North far below.

How big do you think Utuyu would have looked if you were that bird looking down, watching him as he walked up into The Mountains to the North with Ita's children? If you look at that last question I just asked, you'll see a question mark at the end of it. Under the hook on top of the question mark, you'll see a tiny dot. Well, Utuyu wouldn't even have looked nearly as big as that. Of course it was nighttime, too, so that high-flying bird wouldn't have been able to see much of anything at all, not even the mountains, themselves—at least not until the moon came up.

When the moon did come up that night, it was only a little bit of the moon. It looked like it was lying on its back, the way the white part at the end of your fingernails looks when you fold your fingers toward you. There wasn't enough of the moon in the sky yet to give much light, but Utuyu could see the road going on and on, and up and up, and twisting this way and that way. It was the same road Utuyu had traveled along when he came down to Oaxaca from Ita's house, but it certainly looked different to him now. Even in daylight, roads look different when you're going one way than they look when you're coming back the other way. What was in front of you when you were going, ends up being behind you coming back. When it's dark, though, everything looks *really* different.

There was something else about the road up into the mountains that seemed different to Utuyu this time. It didn't make his legs as tired as it had before, no matter that now he was going up instead of coming down. His legs were longer and stronger now. They were used to doing a lot of walking after all the time he'd spent walking around the city every day. No truck came by this time to give anyone a ride in the back, and Utuyu was doing more walking than he'd ever done before. All the same, his legs felt fine.

Everybody stopped when they came to the place with the pond. Utuyu had been asleep in the back of the truck when he'd passed the place on the way to Oaxaca, so he'd never seen it before. Looking at the pond in the darkness, he couldn't imagine people splashing about in the black water. Ita's children had all brought something along to eat, and Utuyu was glad he'd thought about bringing something, too. He was hungry after all that walking.

One of Ita's children said, "Utuyu, sing us a song." The others all said, "Yes, Utuyu! Sing for us!"

Utuyu said, "Okay. But you'll have to pay me money like the people in the big square."

Nobody said anything, not anything at all. There wasn't a sound. For a moment, it seemed darker all around than it had been before.

Utuyu laughed out loud. "Gotcha, didn't I? I was just joking, you nincompoops!" he said.

Then he sang for them. His voice didn't bounce off any walls, like it did when he sang in Father Juan's church, because there weren't any walls for it to bounce off. But Utuyu liked the way his voice sounded out there in the mountains in the middle of the night. He liked the sound just as much as the sound his voice made in the church, although it was different. Here, by the pond, his voice seemed to float away into the night. His song floated off across the pond, through the darkness of the trees the other side, and then his song seemed to rise up out of the darkness, up to the little fingernail moon in the sky. Utuyu felt he could go on singing all night, but after a while, it was time to go on walking up the road some more.

As they went on walking, the sky began to change colors, the way it had when Utuyu had started down the same road from Ita's house on his way to the city. The blackness of the sky became purple-ish, then red-ish, then orange-ish, and then yellow-ish as the sun came up. By the time they reached Ita's house at last, the sky was all blue, and the sun was shining where the moon had been. The sun was big and bright and warm.

There was no one to be seen when they walked across the clearing in front of the house. Clothes were hanging on clotheslines tied to the trees. They reminded Utuyu of the brightly colored clothes hanging out to dry on the roof of the green building the far side of the flat space where he'd lived for a while in Oaxaca. There was a fire burning in front of Ita's house, and on the fire was the big, black, iron pot Utuyu remembered seeing all the time when he lived at Ita's house. It was almost the size of a table, but although it was big, it looked smaller to Utuyu now. Ita's house looked smaller than Utuyu remembered it as well.

"Good morning, Mama!" the children shouted.

Ita came out of her house, followed by a little boy. Utuyu wondered who the little boy was, and then he remembered the baby Ita had been looking after when he'd left for the city. He was certainly no baby now! Ita put her hand up to her eyes so she could see into the early morning sun. She waved to them, and the little boy waved, too. Two of the children ran to her and hugged her around the waist.

"So!" said Ita. "Here you are!" Then she said what Utuyu knew she was going to say next. "Everybody safe and sound?" Ita asked.

The children all nodded.

"Good!" said Ita. "Then get right to work. We've got lots to do for tomorrow."

That's when Ita noticed there was one more child in the group than she'd been expecting. "And who's this you've brought along?" she asked.

For a moment, Utuyu thought Ita didn't know who he was anymore, and for that moment he felt strange, like a stranger. But when Ita squinted her eyes into the sun, she knew who he was all right. "Utuyu!" she said, and her hands flew up in surprise.

"Come here and let me look at you," said Ita.

Utuyu went to her and gave her a hug. Once upon a time, his arms had gone around Ita's knees when he hugged her. Now, his arms went around just under Ita's own arms. Like the iron pot and the house itself, Ita seemed smaller than he remembered.

"Welcome back," Ita said. "And just look at the size of you, will you! There must be plenty of good food down there in Oaxaca for you to have sprouted up like this!"

"I can speak the other language, too," said Utuyu, and he wanted to tell her all about what he'd been doing in the city. Ita stopped him, though.

"Later, later," she said. "You can tell me all about Oaxaca later on. Right now it's time to get wood! Water! To grind corn! You still remember how to grind corn?"

Utuyu nodded. He still remembered.

"Then get going!" Ita said. "There's a lot of corn to grind up."

So that's how Utuyu spent the rest of the morning. The other children went off here and there and came back with armfuls of wood and buckets of water, and he sat in the sun, grinding up the corn just the way he'd done so many times before. This time, though, his arms didn't feel like they might fall off. His arms had grown longer and stronger, like his legs. He felt he could go on grinding corn all day, but when the sun was overhead in the sky and felt as hot as the fire under the old iron pot, Ita told everyone to stop doing what they were doing and to come and get something to eat.

Everybody ate, and then everybody lay down in shady places out of the sun. It didn't take more than a moment for all of Ita's children to fall fast asleep. After all, they'd walked all through the night and then worked half way through the day. Utuyu chose a shady place under a large bush and lay down. His body told him right away it needed some sleep, too. He wanted to think about being back at Ita's house, but he didn't have time to think about what he wanted to think about before his thoughts turned into a dream.

His dream was about being back in the park in Oaxaca where he'd slept under the bushes. It wasn't a good dream, though. The dream bushes in the dream park were too small to hide him. He kept trying to make himself smaller, but the bushes seemed to get smaller instead. There was no way he could stay out of sight of the people walking by. The dream people pointed at him and laughed. One of the people was Gabriel, and Gabriel was pointing and laughing at him, too. When Utuyu looked down at himself in his dream, he could see why everyone was pointing and laughing. His dream shoes had become so small that they only covered his big toe and the toe next to it, and the bottoms of the legs of his dream pants had shrunk up around his knees. Gabriel started clapping his hands and shouting, "Dummy! Dummy!" That's when Utuyu woke up.

It was really Ita who was clapping her hands. She was standing in the doorway of her house, calling to her children, telling them it was time for them to stop sleeping and finish up the work that had to be done. The sun was lower in the sky now. The day wasn't nearly so hot anymore.

This time, it was Utuyu's turn to fetch water from the river. He remembered how hard it had been once for him to bring one pail of water back from the river to Ita's house. Now, he could bring back two pails full, one in each hand. The full pails tugged hard on his shoulders, and the metal handles were hard against the insides of his hands, and he had to walk slowly, but he could do it—without spilling much of the water along the way.

By the time night had come and all the work was done, everybody was ready to go to sleep again. All the children went into the house and lay down on the grass mats on the dirt floor. Utuyu curled up on his side, with his hands under one ear. He listened to the old sounds of the children falling asleep. He could hear their breathing, and now and then some sleepy mumbling and sleepy little snorts.

Just before he fell asleep as well, Utuyu thought about how he used to look up at all the different shaped balloons on the ceiling of his room back in Oaxaca. He uncurled himself on the dirt floor and stretched out on his back, the way he used to do on his old mattress. He had to curl himself right back up again, though, because his legs bumped into someone else. There didn't seem to be as much room on Ita's floor as there used to be.

Chapter Twenty-Seven

The next morning, Utuyu was the last of the children to get up and get going. He wasn't used to sleeping on the hard, dirt floor anymore. His arms and legs wanted more time to go on lying there doing nothing at all. When he woke up, though, there were busy sounds all around him. He could smell the smoke from the fire burning in front of the house. There were new voices calling back and forth that he hadn't heard before. His arms and legs felt tired and stiff, but Utuyu wanted to know what was going on. He was hungry, too, and his nose told him he wouldn't have to go far to find something to eat.

In front of the house the big iron pot was steaming away over its own fire, but now there were other fires as well. Around the clear space, people Utuyu hadn't seen before were sitting around smaller fires of their own. On each of the smaller fires something was cooking.

"Hey!" a man shouted to him. "Over here!"

Utuyu looked to see who was calling. It was a man sitting around his fire with a woman and two children about Utuyu's age. They weren't anyone he knew, but the man waved for him to come over, and Utuyu did. People were going from fire to fire, eating and talking and laughing like they all knew each other, whether they did or not.

"Eat!" said the woman, and she scooped a bowlful of hot, thick, red soup out of her pot and gave it to him. The soup was made of corn and meat and cabbage and radishes. It was spicy and good.

"Where are you from?" asked one of the children.

"Oaxaca," said Utuyu.

They all stopped eating and looked at him.

The man shook his head. "It's crazy down there in Oaxaca city. I wouldn't want to live there. No way."

"It's not so crazy," said Utuyu. "Not once you get to know how things work."

"Do you speak the other language?" asked one of the children.

"Yes," said Utuyu. "I learned how."

"What do people do down there in the city?" asked the woman.

It was hard for Utuyu to find an answer to that question. When he thought about it, there seemed to be a lot of answers he could give.

"They buy and sell things a lot," Utuyu said. "They find things the people want, and the people give them money."

"Things like what?" asked one of the children.

"Like bread and like balloons," Utuyu said.

"What are balloons?" asked the other child.

"They're things on strings," said Utuyu. "They're all different shapes and colors, and they stay up in the air." That was all he could think of to say about balloons.

"What do people do with these balloon things?" one of the children asked. "Can you eat them?"

The woman laughed. "No, silly, you can't eat them! All you can do is look at them."

"See?" said the man. "Like I said, it's crazy down there in Oaxaca city. People pay money for things they can't do anything with. Like balloons."

"Balloons are nice," said Utuyu, but he said it quietly. More quietly still, he said, "I like balloons."

The man said something back, but Utuyu didn't hear what it was. It was like the man was talking to his thick, red soup.

Some parties you and I go to, like birthday parties, for example, go on for a couple of hours, and then everyone goes home. Other parties, like parties when people get married, go on longer. They may go on all night long. This party in the mountains at Ita's house went on longer than that. It went on for three whole days. When people weren't eating and drinking, they were singing and dancing. The quietest times were the times when everyone got together around the big fire, and men took turns talking about things that had happened long ago.

The men told stories about a time when there were only people like themselves, and everyone spoke the same language. They lived in caves far under the ground, and only went up into the sunlight to gather food. They told stories about new people who came, people who lived above the ground and spoke a different language. It rained so hard, and it rained so long up there above the ground that all the new people got washed away. That story reminded Utuyu of a story Father Juan had told him. It was a story about a man who, once upon a time, put his family and lots of animals in a big boat to save them when it rained so hard that water had covered everything.

There were times, too, sitting around the fire telling stories, when the men asked help from the sun, the moon, the winds and the rain. They asked help for making the seeds they planted grow into plants like corn that would give them food. They asked for help in hunting the animals they needed for feeding their families. They said thank you to the fire. They thanked the fire for the light and heat it gave them at night, and they thanked it for cooking all the food they were eating.

All this talk seemed strange to Utuyu. Why didn't these people just go to Oaxaca city, he wondered? In the city, no one had to plant corn or hunt animals. There was food everywhere. If it rained hard, no one got washed away. They opened their umbrellas or stood under the arches around the big square. When it got dark, no one needed a fire to see where they were going. The lights on tall posts went on all by themselves.

Several of the men had brought musical instruments to the party. The first night of the party, one man began singing, and then two others joined in with violins. Someone started playing a drum, and someone else a guitar. One man took a harmonica out of his pocket and started playing that as well. When the men were playing all together at once, the sound of the violins was the clearest sound of all. It wasn't a loud sound, but it rose above the sounds of the other instruments, as if someone was singing. Utuyu wondered if anyone was going to play a trumpet, like the men in the big square in Oaxaca did, but no one had brought a trumpet along.

That first night, one of Ita's children said to everybody, "Utuyu can sing! He sings in Oaxaca, and the people give him money to do it!"

"So sing for us!" everybody said to Utuyu. Then they all stopped talking and looked at him.

Utuyu didn't have time to think about what song he would sing to these people, so when he began singing, his song was one of the ones he liked singing best in Father Juan's church. It was one of the happier songs, and, of course, it was in the new language.

Everybody listened quietly. When he had finished, no one said anything. They looked at one another, and nodded their heads. Some people shrugged their shoulders. They smiled at Utuyu, and then one of the men began playing his violin once more. The others took up their instruments and joined in, singing an old song in the old language.

No one asked Utuyu to sing again—not then, and not during all the time that the party lasted.

Finally, after the second night, it was time for everyone to go home. The men took their hammocks down from the trees and packed up their musical instruments. The women gathered up their pots, wrapped up their blankets and clothes, and rounded up their children. The people said goodbye to Ita and to one another, and with their bundles on their heads and on their backs, they walked off into the trees the way they had come three days before. When the last person had left, it seemed very quiet at Ita's house, even with all of Ita's children still there.

The children stayed at Ita's house for several more days, helping her with things that needed to be done. They cleared the bushes away from a small space near the house and dug up the earth so that Ita could plant seeds. Utuyu helped as best he could, but he didn't know much about digging. Breaking up the ground was tough work, too. The ground was dry and hard now, but when the rains came, it would get soft again, and the seeds would grow into plants that would give Ita new things to eat.

Utuyu went on digging until there were places on his hands that were so sore that he had to stop. After that, he helped make a fence around the space the children had cleared. The fence was made out of twigs and small branches all twisted together. It would keep animals, like rabbits and such, from eating the new plants before they turned into the vegetables Ita wanted. The twigs and branches had to be twisted together in a certain way so that the animals couldn't get through them. Utuyu didn't know how to do the twisting, so his job was to find the right-sized twigs and branches for the other children to use.

The roof of Ita's house needed some fixing, too. There were places on it that would let the rain in when it came. The roof was made of leaves, and pieces of tin, and strong reeds that grew by the river. Two of the older children climbed up on the roof and seemed to know just how to put everything in place to keep the rain out. Utuyu started to climb up on the roof to help, but the children who were up there told him to climb back down.

"You don't know how to do this," they said. "You're a boy from the city, and city boys don't know about these things. Just get us some more reeds." So that's what Utuyu did for the rest of the day.

One night not long after Ita's roof was fixed, Utuyu saw that Ita's children were packing up their things and getting ready to leave.

"We're going back to Oaxaca for while," one of the children told him. "You coming with us?"

Utuyu shook his head. "No," he said. "I'm going to stay here now. I'm not going back to Oaxaca."

"You can't stay here forever, you know," said one of the children. "Ita won't let you."

That was something Utuyu hadn't thought about before.

"Then I'll go somewhere else," he said.

"Like where?" asked another of the children.

Utuyu didn't have an answer for that, so he didn't say anything.

Early the next morning, while it was still dark, Utuyu heard the children leave. He stayed right where he was, curled up on the floor, and pretended he was still asleep. Ita was already up and about, giving her children food to take with them on their long walk to Oaxaca. Out of the corner of one eye, Utuyu watched her wave goodbye to them from outside the doorway. Then Ita came back into the house.

Lying there on the floor, Utuyu could only see Ita's bare feet. When he saw her feet stop right next to him, he shut his eyes tight. He wondered if she was going to say something to him, but she didn't. When he opened his eyes again, just a tiny bit, her feet weren't there anymore.

Chapter Twenty-Eight

Each day seemed to get hotter than the last one. In the early mornings, Utuyu went to the river to fetch water. He didn't really have to anymore, because the cement box in the ground where Ita kept her water stayed nearly full. Ita didn't use much water every day. Utuyu used less that Ita did, and Ita's little boy used hardly any water at all.

Before the sun was up in the sky, making the day too hot to want to do anything, Utuyu ground up more of the corn Ita had put aside in big bags. Soon, he had ground up enough corn to last for many days. Ita didn't eat much of the flat bread she made, and he didn't eat much, either. Ita's little boy ate hardly any at all. When the time came to eat each day, the day was so hot that no one felt hungry. Besides, it was too hot to do the busy kinds of things that make people feel hungry.

Everything in the world seemed to slow down. During the days, Utuyu didn't see as many rabbits and squirrels around as he'd seen before. The few rabbits he did see weren't hopping about anymore. They stayed in one place, in the shade of the bushes. When they were nibbling on the little bits of grass they could find, they looked like they were nibbling in their sleep. The squirrels walked slowly along the branches of the trees, instead of jumping from limb to limb. They hardly flicked their tails up and down the way squirrels usually do.

Utuyu had lots of time to wonder what to do with himself. He went to the place in the rocks where he knew the scorpions lived and tried to get two scorpions to fight each other. They didn't seem to want to fight. Scorpions like hot places, and it was certainly hot there in the rocky place, hotter than anywhere else, but the scorpions acted as if they couldn't be bothered to fight. When Utuyu pushed one of them harder with the stick, it didn't even try to sting. *Go about your business and leave us be. You don't belong here,* it seemed to say. That was no help to Utuyu at all, because he couldn't think of any business to go about, and if he didn't belong there, where *did* he belong?

A hawk went by overhead while Utuyu was there in the rocks. It didn't move its wings at all, but hawks usually don't move their wings much, whether it's hot or not. Utuyu thought that this particular hawk looked different, though. He thought it looked lazy and bored. He could imagine it up there in the sky, yawning, because there was nothing for it to see moving around down below.

I don't think that hawks really know what it means to feel bored, and I don't think they know how to yawn. They don't have feelings like people do, and so I don't think they know what it feels like to wander around wondering what to do next, when it seems that there's nothing at all to do. If you ask me, I think that Utuyu was the one who was feeling bored and wondering what to do next, and so he imagined the hawk feeling the same way. That's what I think.

The nights stayed hot, too. They stayed hot, and they were quieter than usual, as though the night animals found it too hot to whirr or whistle or chirp. A full moon came up one night. It seemed to be giving off heat, which, of course the moon never does, but it was so big and bright that it seemed to be what was making the night air so warm.

Utuyu lay on his back outside Ita's house and stared up at the moon. When you stare at the moon when it's full, you may think the shadows from the mountains up there on the moon make shapes that look something like a man's face. To Utuyu, the shapes of the shadows on the moon looked more like a rabbit. That imaginary rabbit on the moon looked like it was asleep in the heat of the night. Like everything else around, that rabbit seemed to be waiting for something to happen.

The full moon made Utuyu think about Father Juan, and what he was doing down there in Oaxaca. Thinking about Father Juan made him think about Señora Blanca, about the woman who sold bread, and about the balloon man. What were they all doing right now? Thinking about the balloon man made Utuyu wonder if someone else was looking after the balloons at night now. He thought about all the balloons in the big square, and about the people sitting at their tables, and about the men and women in black and white coming and going, and about the sound of the trumpet that would be floating around the big square, floating above all the rest of the sounds in the square.

All of Utuyu's thoughts about the city turned into a question in his mind. Were all these things he remembered in Oaxaca really still going on, even though he wasn't there to see them or hear them? Or was it as quiet now in Oaxaca as it was here at Ita's house? Lying there in the hot, still night, he stared at the shadowy rabbit on the moon and wondered about that.

Late one afternoon, Utuyu was sitting in the shade looking at the shapes that dark clouds were making over the distant mountains. There didn't used to be clouds there at all, but now they turned up every afternoon. Some looked only like taller mountains, but often they turned into birds, or snakes, or people's faces. Every now and then there would be a quick flash of lightning in the clouds, but the clouds were so far away that the flash looked like a tiny spark in the dark ashes of a fire.

While he was sitting there looking at the clouds that afternoon, Ita came out of her house. She walked toward him, carrying a basket of fruit and a sharp knife. From the way she was scowling, Utuyu could tell she had something on her mind. He hoped what was on her mind was something for him to do, because he was running out of things to think up for himself.

Ita squatted down beside him and began peeling the fruit. "You should go before the rains come," she said.

That wasn't what Utuyu had expected Ita to say right then, but when she said it, it was like she'd said something he'd known she was going to say sooner or later.

"Back to the city?" Utuyu asked, but of course he knew that's what Ita meant.

Ita nodded. "You don't belong here," she said. She didn't say it unkindly. The way she said it was like she might have been saying something simple and ordinary, like, "It's hot today," or "It's getting late."

"I don't know where I belong," Utuyu said.

Ita thought about that for a moment, and then she said, "Where does the river belong?"

Utuyu frowned. *Grownups say such strange things!* he thought. How was he supposed to answer a question like "Where does the river belong?"

"I don't know," he said. "It belongs where it is, I guess."

"Yes," Ita said. "Right where it is. And does the water stay in the same place all the time?"

Utuyu shook his head. Of course it didn't.

"So where does the water belong?" Ita asked.

Now Utuyu really didn't know what he was supposed to say. "It belongs wherever it goes, I guess," he said.

"See how smart you are?" Ita said, but Utuyu didn't feel like he'd said anything smart at all.

"The water doesn't worry about where it belongs," Ita said. "It goes wherever the river takes it, and wherever the river takes the water, the water belongs there."

Utuyu felt he was beginning to understand a little bit of what Ita was saying—not all of it, but at least a little bit of it. It was like when Señora Blanca had talked to him about the legs of his pants getting too short and having to add new pieces at the bottom.

"So what am I supposed to do?" he said.

"The river has taken you to the city," said Ita, "and because it has, that's where you belong now. One day, maybe it will take you somewhere else, and then you'll belong in that place, too."

Utuyu looked around him. He looked at Ita's house and the new patches on the roof he had helped the children make. He looked at the clear space around the house and at the new ground he'd helped the children dig for the new plants Ita would grow. He looked at the distant mountains and the dark clouds that went on changing their shapes above them.

"You've always been here," he said to Ita.

"Yes," Ita said. "I belong here."

"The river didn't take you anywhere," Utuyu said. "How come?"

"There are quiet places in the river, too," Ita said. "A river needs places where the water can stay quiet. But even in the quiet places, the water changes."

"I like it here," Utuyu said.

"That's good," said Ita. "It's good to like the place you come from. We are your people. We have always been here. We will still be here whenever you want to come back and remember where you came from, too."

"I can come back no matter where the river takes me?" asked Utuyu.

"Yes," said Ita. "You are luckier than the water in the river. The water can never go back to where it started, but you can."

Utuyu stayed at Ita's house for two more days. After his talk with Ita, he felt better about going back to the city. He felt better about it, but he still needed a little more time to feel altogether good about it. During those two days, he spent more and more time thinking about what his life had been like in Oaxaca. He began wanting to see the streets and the buildings again. He wanted to hear the sounds of the city again, and to smell the city's own particular smells. He wanted to sing to the people again, and to talk the new language again. He felt as if he'd left part of himself down there in the city, without knowing he'd left anything behind. He felt he needed to go back and find that part of himself again, to put himself back together in one piece.

Utuyu left Ita's house when the sun was low in the sky. The road down the mountain was already in shadow. Ita had given him enough food to eat on the way, and even more food than that, so he knew he would have enough to eat the next day as well. As he was wrapping up his bundle of things to take with him, he came across his bag of money. He'd forgotten all about it.

Utuyu took the bag of money to Ita and gave it to her.

"Here," he said. "You use it."

"Thank you," Ita said. "That will come in handy. But you keep some of it. You'll need it in the city."

"You can keep it all," Utuyu said. "I know how to get more any time I want some."

When he and Ita said goodbye, it was a good goodbye. He felt good now about going to the city. He knew he had a place at Ita's house he could always come back to again. He felt it was all right to try new things and do new things, because there was a place in The Mountains to the North where part of him would always belong.

Chapter Twenty-Nine

Utuyu is still in the city of Oaxaca. I know that, because I saw him there not long ago.

You may wonder how I came to know so much about Utuyu, about where he came from, and how he got to the city, and about what he did there. I've been able to tell you all that, because I often go to Oaxaca myself, and Utuyu is a friend of mine. He told me everything I've told you.

The last time I saw Utuyu, I was sitting at a table under the arches in the big square. He was walking by, and he stopped to sit with me for a while. When I first met him, he hadn't been in the city long. It was nighttime, and he was singing to the people at the tables. I don't remember what he was wearing then, but I remember he looked like a grubby little boy who had been wearing the same clothes for days and days and days. This time, when he came to sit at my table and talk to me, he was wearing clean, dark-blue pants, a clean white shirt, and a bright red sweater without sleeves. He told me his clothes were what everyone has to wear at the school he's going to now. He still didn't know exactly how old he was, but we figured out that he must be about ten or 11.

We talked together in the new language Utuyu had learned. It's called Spanish, and it's not the language my people spoke when I was growing up. I had to learn

Spanish as a new language, too, just like Utuyu did. Utuyu speaks Spanish now much better than I do, and I like it when he tells me how to say something right in Spanish when I say it wrong—which I often do. Utuyu helps me keep on learning.

Now, we can also talk together in my own language, which of course is called English. We can't say a whole lot to each other in English yet, because Utuyu has just begun learning my language. I like it when I can help him keep on learning, just the way he can help me.

What we can't do is talk together in Utuyu's own language. It's a very difficult language for anybody to learn who didn't learn it when they were small. When he and I are together, and we meet some of Utuyu's own people, he has to tell me what they are saying. I think he likes doing that. I think he likes knowing something I don't know.

Utuyu has shown me the doorway where he spent his first night in Oaxaca. That was the night he woke up and his balloon was gone. He's taken me to the little park where he slept under the bushes for a while, and to the flat space where he lived next. As I've told you already, there are buildings there now, and it isn't a flat space anymore. The old, yellow building is still there across the street, though, and when we went there together, the brown dog with the white face was up there on the roof, barking at everyone who was going by. He even barked at Utuyu.

"I don't think he remembers me anymore," Utuyu said. "I think I look different now."

Thanks to Utuyu, I've met Señora Blanca and the balloon man as well. Señora Blanca is still teaching at the school where Utuyu began learning Spanish. Utuyu showed me the classroom where he sat, and the chair he used to sit in. The chair is too small for him now, and he looked funny when he showed me how he used to sit in it.

While I was talking to Señora Blanca, she said, "When Utuyu went back to the mountains, the teachers thought that maybe we'd lost him for good, and that we'd never see him again. I didn't think so, though. I thought he'd come back. I'm glad he did."

Utuyu told me he still goes to Señora Blanca's school now and then. He told me he helps the new kids find their way around, and can help some of them learn Spanish.

"Part of you still belongs at Señora Blanca's school, doesn't it?" I asked him.

"Yes," Utuyu said, and I could tell from the way he said it that he was happy about that.

The balloon man was still sitting in his wooden box on the street when we went to the place where Utuyu had lived and looked after the balloons at night.

"Hey, kid!" the balloon man shouted when we got there. "You're looking pretty cool in those fancy clothes! Who's this you've got with you?"

"A friend of mine," said Utuyu. "I want to show him where I used to live."

"Well, you just go right ahead and do that," said the balloon man. Then the balloon man said to me, "This one is the best kid I ever had looking after my balloons. The others, they come and go, and I never know if they're going to turn up or not, or if they're going to stay around or not. Now when I was a kid," he said, "things were different. If you were lucky enough to get a job, you did whatever you had to do to keep that job, 'cause there weren't many jobs around. Nowadays . . . ."

Just then, two cars drove up to the wooden box, and the drivers wanted the balloon man to let them in.

"Know what I mean?" said the balloon man, and then he started tearing off the pieces of paper the drivers would need to get their cars back out later on.

"He talks a lot, doesn't he?" Utuyu said to me.

"Yes," I said. "Some people seem to need to do that."

It wasn't a Sunday, and so I didn't get to meet the woman who sold bread. Utuyu didn't think it was a good idea to go to her house, and so we didn't. But he goes there often after school. He's helping one of her children learn to read and write. We did go to meet Father Juan, though. He was at his church, and he was pleased to see Utuyu. Father Juan made me feel welcome, too. He asked me to come and hear Utuyu sing in his church sometime, and I did that. Utuyu has a beautiful voice. When he sings, his voice fills the big room inside the church. When he's singing, everyone listens very quietly.

"I like singing there," Utuyu said. "It's the only time I get to sing anymore. I don't sing to the people in the big square the way I did before. I haven't got the time at night now. I have to do a lot of things to get ready for school."

Then Utuyu said, "Father Juan asked me again if I wanted to get a new name. He thinks I should, but I don't know. What do you think?"

"Well," I said, "if you want to some day, you can. But I think I'll always call you Utuyu. It would feel funny calling you something else."

"That's kind of how I feel about it," Utuyu said. "And I still can't figure out why someone would need another name, anyway."

While we were sitting at the table when I was in Oaxaca that last time, I asked Utuyu where he was living now. He told me he was living in the same place he'd gone to live when he came back from the mountains and started going to the new school. It's a nice house, Utuyu said, and he likes living there. The house has enough rooms in it so that he has a room of his own. When he feels like it, he told me, he can close the door and be by himself.

"The woman who lives there is kind of strict about things," Utuyu told me. "She wants me to be there at certain times, and there are lots of things she makes me do to keep the place looking the way she wants it to look. She gets mad if I mess things up. She's kind of like Ita, but she's different."

I said I thought that it must have been hard for him to get used to living in such a new sort of place, not being able to do whatever he felt like. Utuyu said that, at the beginning, it had been, but that he'd gotten used to it.

"One of the hardest things for me to get used to," he said, "was getting used to sleeping up in the air on a bed." Then he told me about one of his first nights in the new house. He'd climbed up onto the bed and gone to sleep. In his sleep, he'd had a dream.

"I dreamt I was back in my old room looking after the balloons again," Utuyu said. "It wasn't a good dream, because everything in the room, like the pieces of old cars and stuff, was moving around. The balloons on the ceiling were moving around, too. It was like everything was worried about something.

"There were voices outside, and I thought maybe the balloons were worried that they were going to get stolen or something. I wanted to stop the people outside coming in, but I couldn't get up off my mattress on the floor. I was kind of stuck there."

"I know that kind of dream," I said to Utuyu. "There's something in the dream you really need to do, but you can't do it. I still have those dreams sometimes. I don't like them at all. So what happened next in your dream?" I asked him.

"Well," he said, "the whole room started kind of shaking. I knew the balloons were trying to get away from the people outside, but I couldn't help them. Then the balloons pushed so hard against the ceiling that the room came loose from the ground. It went up in the air, and me along with it."

"That must have been scary!" I said.

"It was to start with," Utuyu said, "but we'd gotten away from whoever the people were, and that felt good. We were kind of flying around up there in the sky, and I crawled over to a window and looked out."

"Could you see anything?" I asked.

"I could see Ita's children way down below, and they were shouting something to me. I leaned out the window to hear what they were shouting, and then I was falling through the air, and that *was* scary! And then, POOM! I hit the ground. And I really did. I woke up on the floor next to my bed."

"You'd fallen off your bed?" I asked.

"Right off it," Utuyu said. "Right onto the floor. Just like that!"

I laughed.

"I know, it's kind of funny now," Utuyu said, "but it wasn't funny then."

"No," I said. "I'm sure it wasn't."

"I didn't tell anyone, but I slept on the floor for a lot of nights after that," Utuyu said. "I wasn't sure the bed would let me stay on it all night."

"But you tried again and got used to it?" I asked him.

"What I did was go and buy a balloon," Utuyu told me. "I bought one of the balloons in the big square that looks like a dog. I took it home with me and let it stay up against the ceiling above the bed. With the string hanging down where I could reach it when I was on the bed. Then I tried sleeping on the bed again, and it was all right."

"And then you got used to sleeping up there," I said.

"Sort of," Utuyu said. "But I still always keep a balloon up there. And before I go to sleep, I pretend I'm back on my mattress on the floor at the balloon man's place, looking up at the balloons. Then it's okay."

After he'd told me about his dream, Utuyu looked at his watch. Yes, he had his own watch now. He said it was six thirty, and he had to get home to do the things he had to do to get ready for school the next morning. I was sorry to see him go, because I liked hearing about everything that was going on in his life. It seems to me that he's found ways to do a lot of things that must have seemed hard for him when he had to do them for the first time. He's certainly learned a lot, that's for sure. I'm glad that he had people who cared about him and who wanted to help him.

I'll see Utuyu again, I know. I'll look for him the next time I go to Oaxaca. He asked me to go with him one day up into The Mountains to the North, to Ita's house. I'd like to do that, but I told him I didn't think I could walk that far.

"We won't have to walk," he said. "You can rent a car." Utuyu certainly knows a lot about how things work now, doesn't he?

I told him that if we went up into the mountains, I wouldn't understand anything anyone was saying up there.

"That's okay," he said. "They're my people. I know what they're saying. I can tell you."

When Utuyu and I go to Ita's house together, it will all be strange and new to me. I'm glad I'll have the "Sky Boy" along to help me.

About the Illustrator

Noël Dora Chilton, founder of the Sachmo Art Center in Oaxaca, is the illustrator of many children's stories both about Oaxaca and beyond. "I really empathized with Utuyu," she says. "Growing up, I always seemed to be starting again in a new place. Then I came to Mexico in 1999, not knowing Spanish or anything about the country." Since then, Noël has married a Oaxaqueño, become the mother of two children, and continues her own artwork while maintaining a busy schedule of classes and exhibitions at Sachmo. "Viva new challenges!" she says. "Viva Utuyu!"